1. The Old Woman of Kilburn Lane and the Butcher of Parc Monceau

Joseph, the office boy, made the faintest of noises, barely that of a scurrying mouse, as he scratched at the door. Inching it open so that it didn't creak, he then slipped so silently into Maigret's office that, with the halo of white, almost translucent hair around his otherwise bald head, he might have been pretending to be a ghost.

Maigret was bent over some files, pipe stem clamped between his teeth. He did not look up, and Joseph remained rooted to the spot.

Maigret had been on edge, and his colleagues had been tiptoeing in and out of his office for a week. And he wasn't the only one, either in Paris or anywhere else in France; no one had ever known such a damp, cold, gloomy March.

At eleven in the morning the office still looked like the morning of a hanging. The lights were kept blazing past noon, and dusk started to fall at three. They couldn't tell if it was raining any more, since they were actually living inside a rain cloud, with water everywhere, trails of it on the floors and people unable to say three words to anyone without blowing their noses.

The newspapers carried photographs of commuters going home by boat on streets that might as well have been rivers.

When he got to work in the morning, Maigret would ask:

'Is Janvier here?'

'Sick.'

'Lucas?'

'His wife rang to say . . .'

His inspectors came down with the flu one by one, sometimes in whole batches, so that his team was never more than at a third of its full strength.

Madame Maigret, meanwhile, hadn't caught the flu. She had a toothache. Every night, despite the dentist's best efforts, it came on around two or three in the morning, and she wouldn't close her eyes again until it was almost dawn.

She was brave, never complained, never let out so much as a groan.

But that only made the whole thing worse. Suddenly, in mid-sleep, Maigret would become aware that she was awake. He would feel her holding in her moans so fiercely that she hardly dared breathe. He wouldn't say anything for a while. He would just lie there, spying on her suffering, as it were, until finally he wouldn't be able to help muttering:

'Why don't you take a pill?'

'Aren't you asleep?'

'No. Take a pill.'

'You know they don't do anything any more.'

'Take one anyway.'

He would get out of bed, barefoot, go and fetch the packet, and then give it to her with a glass of water without being able to hide how tired and increasingly irritated he was.

'Extraordinary masterpieces of the twentieth century'
– John Banville

'A brilliant writer'   – India Knight

'Intense atmosphere and resonant detail . . . make Simenon's
fiction remarkably like life'   – Julian Barnes

'A truly wonderful writer . . . marvellously readable – lucid,
simple, absolutely in tune with the world he creates'
– Muriel Spark

'Few writers have ever conveyed with such a sure touch, the
bleakness of human life'   – A. N. Wilson

'Compelling, remorseless, brilliant'   – John Gray

'A writer of genius, one whose simplicity of language creates
indelible images that the florid stylists of our own day can
only dream of'   – *Daily Mail*

'The mysteries of the human personality are revealed in all
their disconcerting complexity'   – Anita Brookner

'One of the greatest writers of our time'   – *The Sunday Times*

'I love reading Simenon. He makes me think of Chekhov'
– William Faulkner

'One of the great psychological novelists of this century'
– *Independent*

'The greatest of all, the most genuine novelist we have had
in literature'   – André Gide

'Simenon ought to be spoken of in the same breath as
Camus, Beckett and Kafka'   – *Independent on Sunday*

ABOUT THE AUTHOR

Georges Simenon was born on 12 February 1903 in Liège, Belgium, and died in 1989 in Lausanne, Switzerland, where he had lived for the latter part of his life. Between 1931 and 1972 he published seventy-five novels and twenty-eight short stories featuring Inspector Maigret.

Simenon always resisted identifying himself with his famous literary character, but acknowledged that they shared an important characteristic:

> My motto, to the extent that I have one, has been noted often enough, and I've always conformed to it. It's the one I've given to old Maigret, who resembles me in certain points . . . 'understand and judge not'.

Penguin is publishing the entire series of Maigret novels.

GEORGES SIMENON

Maigret's Failure

Translated by WILLIAM HOBSON

PENGUIN BOOKS

PENGUIN CLASSICS

UK | USA | Canada | Ireland | Australia
India | New Zealand | South Africa

Penguin Books is part of the Penguin Random House group of companies
whose addresses can be found at global.penguinrandomhouse.com

First published in French as *Un échec de Maigret* by Presses de la Cité 1956
This translation first published 2017
002

Set in 12.5/15 pt Dante MT Std
Typeset by Jouve (UK), Milton Keynes
Printed in Great Britain by Clays Ltd, St Ives plc

ISBN: 978–0–241–30378–8

www.greenpenguin.co.uk

MIX
Paper from
responsible sources
FSC® C018179

Penguin Random House is committed to a
sustainable future for our business, our readers
and our planet. This book is made from Forest
Stewardship Council® certified paper.

Contents

Contents

'I'm sorry,' she'd sigh.

'It's not your fault.'

'I can always go and sleep in the maid's room.'

They had one on the sixth floor, which they almost never used.

'Let me go and sleep up there.'

'No.'

'You'll be tired tomorrow and you've got so much to do!'

He had more worries, strictly speaking, than actual work, since this was the moment the old Englishwoman, Mrs Muriel Britt, had chosen to go missing, and it was all over the newspapers.

Women disappear every day, and most of the time it quietly plays itself out. They're found or not, as the case may be, and the newspapers give it three lines at the most.

Muriel Britt's disappearance, however, had caused a storm of publicity, because she had come to Paris with fifty-two other people, an entire train-carriage load, one of those herds of tourists that travel companies round up in England, the United States, Canada or elsewhere and ferry round Paris for a pittance.

It was the evening the group had done 'Paris by night'. A coach had shunted the assortment of mainly middle-aged men and women around Les Halles, Pigalle, Rue de Lappe and the Champs-Élysées, having first equipped them with tickets entitling them to a drink at every establishment they visited.

By the end, everyone was very merry, a sea of ruddy cheeks and shining eyes. A little gentleman with a waxed moustache, a bookkeeper in the City, went missing before the last stop but he was found the following afternoon in his bed, to which he had discreetly retired.

Mrs Britt was a different matter. The English newspapers stressed that she had no reason to disappear. She was fifty-eight years old. Thin and wiry, with the worn-out face and body of a woman who had worked all her life, she ran a boarding house on Kilburn Lane, somewhere in the west of London.

Maigret had no idea what Kilburn Lane was like. Going by the photographs in the newspapers, he pictured a drab establishment inhabited by typists and clerks who would gather at a round table at meal times.

Mrs Britt was a widow. She had a son in South Africa and a married daughter somewhere on the Suez Canal. The papers made a point of stressing that this was the first real holiday the poor woman had treated herself to in her life.

A trip to Paris, where else! In a group. Fixed price, all in. She had been staying with her fellow tourists in a hotel by Gare Saint-Lazare which specialized in these sorts of 'tours'.

She had left the coach at the same time as the rest of the party and gone back to her room. Three witnesses had heard her close the door. The next day she wasn't there, and no trace of her had been found since.

An embarrassed-looking sergeant had arrived from the Yard, made himself known to Maigret, then discreetly set about making his own inquiries.

Meanwhile, less discreetly, the English papers had set about trumpeting the inefficiency of the French police.

But there were certain details that Maigret was loath

to reveal to the press. The fact, for instance, that bottles of alcohol had been found stashed all over Mrs Britt's room: under the mattress, beneath her underwear in a drawer, even on top of the mirrored wardrobe. Or that the grocer who had sold her them had come to Quai des Orfèvres almost the moment her photograph had appeared in an evening paper.

'Did you think there was anything odd about her?'

'Hmm . . . She was tipsy, the wine had obviously been flowing . . . If it was in fact wine. Going on what she bought from me, gin was her tipple . . .'

Had Mrs Britt made a habit of indulging in similarly copious, secret libations in the boarding house on Kilburn Lane? The English newspapers scrupulously avoided saying anything on the subject.

The night porter at the hotel had also given a statement.

'I saw her come creeping back downstairs. She was four sheets to the wind and made a pass at me.'

'Did she go out?'

'Yes.'

'Which way?'

'I don't know.'

A policeman had seen her hesitating outside a bar on Rue d'Amsterdam.

Then that was it. No bodies had been fished out of the Seine. No women had been found chopped up into pieces on a patch of waste ground. Superintendent Pike of the Yard, whom Maigret knew well, rang every morning from London.

'*Sorry*, Maigret. Still no leads?'

That, the rain, his damp clothes, the umbrellas dripping in every corner and, to cap it all, Madame Maigret's teeth made for a pretty unpleasant state of affairs, and Maigret's team could feel he was just waiting for a chance to explode.

'What is it, Joseph?'

'The chief would like a word with you, detective chief inspector.'

'I'll be right there.'

It wasn't time for the daily briefing. When the head of the Police Judiciaire called Maigret into his office during the day like this, it generally meant something significant was up.

He nonetheless finished working on a file, filled a fresh pipe, then headed for the chief's door.

'Still nothing, Maigret?'

He merely shrugged.

'I've just got a letter from the minister by messenger.'

When anyone just said the minister, they meant the minister of the interior, to whom the Police Judiciaire was accountable.

'I'm listening.'

'Someone's coming here at eleven thirty . . .'

It was 11.15.

'A man called Fumal, who is apparently a big shot in his line. At the last elections, he poured God knows how many millions into the party's coffers . . .'

'What has his daughter done?'

'He hasn't got a daughter.'

'His son then.'

'He hasn't got a son either. The minister doesn't say what it's about. Apparently this gentleman just wants to see you in person and you've got to pull out all the stops to keep him happy.'

Maigret mouthed something, a word clearly beginning with an 's'.

'I'm sorry, old friend. I realize too that it's bound to be a chore of some sort or other. But give it your all. We've had enough problems recently.'

Maigret stopped at Joseph's desk in the waiting room.

'When this Fumal character gets here, send him straight in.'

'This who?'

'Fumal! That's his name.'

A name, incidentally, that reminded him of something. Strangely he would have sworn that it was something unpleasant, but he had enough troubles as it was without dredging his memories for more.

'Is Aillevard here?' he asked, standing in the doorway of the inspectors' office.

'He didn't come in this morning.'

'Is he sick?'

'He hasn't rung.'

Janvier, meanwhile, had returned to work, his nose still red, his complexion as grey as rubber.

'How are the kids?'

'Down with flu, naturally.'

Five minutes later there was another scratch at the door, and Joseph announced, as if he was using a slightly off-colour phrase:

'Monsieur Fumal.'

Without looking at his visitor, Maigret muttered:

'Have a seat.'

When he raised his head, he saw a huge, doughy figure who could barely squeeze into the chair. Fumal was looking at him with a mischievous glint, as if he expected Maigret to react in a particular way.

'What's this concerning? I was told you wanted to talk to me personally.'

There were only a few drops of rain on the overcoat of his visitor, who must have come by car.

'Don't you recognize me?'

'No.'

'Think.'

'I don't have time.'

'Ferdinand.'

'Ferdinand what?'

'Fat Ferdinand . . . Boom-Boom!'

Suddenly Maigret remembered. He'd been right in thinking just now that it had unpleasant associations. It was a very old memory, from the time he was at his village school in Saint-Fiacre in the Allier and Mademoiselle Chaigné was the teacher.

In those days Maigret's father was the estate manager at Saint-Fiacre chateau, while Ferdinand was the son of the butcher at Quatre-Vents, a hamlet a kilometre away.

There's always a boy like him in every class: taller and fatter than everyone else, almost morbidly fat.

'Have you got it now?'

'I've got it.'

'What's it like seeing me again? I knew you'd become a cop because I've seen your photo in the papers. Hey, we used to be on first-name terms.'

'Not any more,' Maigret said flatly as he emptied his pipe.

'Up to you. Have you read the minister's letter?'

'No.'

'Hasn't anyone told you anything?'

'They have.'

'We've done pretty well, us two, all things considered. We've followed different paths, of course. My father wasn't an estate manager, was he, he was just a simple village butcher. I was thrown out of Moulins lycée after second year . . .'

His attitude was palpably aggressive, which can't have been solely to do with Maigret. He was the sort of man who would be hard and antagonistic towards everyone, life itself, the heavens above.

'Which didn't stop Oscar telling me today . . .'

Oscar being the minister of the interior.

'. . . "Go and see Maigret. He's the man for you, he'll put himself entirely at your disposal . . . At any rate, I'll see he does . . ."'

Maigret didn't react, just carried on staring his visitor stolidly in the face.

'I remember your father very well,' continued Fumal. 'He had a reddish blond moustache, didn't he? He was thin . . . narrow-chested . . . They must have cooked up some good schemes together, him and my dad . . .'

Maigret had trouble remaining impassive this time;

9

Fumal had hit a raw nerve, one of the most painful memories of his childhood.

Like many country butchers, Fumal's father, who was called Louis, was also to all intents and purposes a cattle dealer. He had gone so far as to rent a few low-lying meadows, where he put the cows to pasture, and gradually expanded across the whole region.

His wife, Ferdinand's mother, was known as 'la belle Fernande'. People said she never wore underwear, and even cynically explained, 'You might miss your chance while you're fiddling about getting them off.'

Are there patches of shadow like this in everyone's childhood memories?

As estate manager, Evariste Maigret was responsible for selling the chateau's cattle. For a long time he had refused to do business with Louis Fumal. But one day he changed his mind, and Fumal had come to the office with his worn wallet stuffed as full of notes as ever.

Maigret must have been seven or eight at the time and he hadn't gone to school, not because of a dose of flu that time, like Janvier's children, but because he had mumps. His mother was still alive. It was very hot in the kitchen and all grey outside, with clear water running down the windowpanes.

His father had rushed in without a hat, which was unusual for him, with drops of rain on his moustache, very agitated.

'That crook Fumal . . .' he had muttered.

'What's he done?'

'I didn't see straight away . . . When he left I put the

money in the safe, then I made a telephone call, and it was only afterwards that I noticed he had slipped two notes under my tobacco jar . . .'

How much was it? All these years later Maigret didn't have a clue, but he vividly remembered his father's anger, his humiliation . . .

'I'm going to chase after him . . .'

'He drove off in his cart?'

'Yes. I'll catch him up on my bicycle and . . .'

The rest was hazy. But after that Fumal's name was only ever mentioned in the house in a particular tone of voice, and the two men never acknowledged one another again. Later there was another, even more obscure incident. Apparently Fumal had tried to make the count of Saint-Fiacre (the old count, that is) suspicious of his estate manager, and Maigret's father had been forced to defend himself.

'I'm listening.'

'Have you heard of me since school?'

Ferdinand Fumal's voice now contained a vague threat.

'No.'

'Do you know "United Butchers"?'

'By name.'

It was a meat wholesaler with shops pretty much everywhere – there was one on Boulevard Voltaire, not far from Maigret's apartment. Small butchers had protested in vain against its expansion.

'That's me. Have you heard of "Bargain Meats"?'

Vaguely. Another 'chain' in more working-class areas and the suburbs.

'That's me too,' Fumal said, with a defiant look. 'Do you know how many millions those two businesses are worth?'

'I'm not interested.'

'I am in charge of "Northern Butchers" too – their head office is in Lille – and "Associated Butchers", whose offices are in Rue Rambuteau.'

Sizing up the bulk of the man wedged in his chair, Maigret almost muttered, 'That's a lot of meat.' But he didn't. He sensed this would prove to be a much more tiresome business than Mrs Britt's disappearance. He already loathed Fumal, and not just for his father's sake. The man was too sure of himself, contemptuously self-confident in a way that was insulting to ordinary people.

Yet you could also sense a certain anxiety under this exterior, perhaps even panic.

'Aren't you going to ask why I'm here?'

'No.'

That was how you drove people like that insane: meet their every move with absolute calm, the force of inertia. There wasn't a flicker of curiosity or interest in Maigret's gaze, and his visitor was starting to get angry.

'Do you know I've got enough clout to get a senior policeman transferred?'

'Ah.'

'Even someone who thinks he's a big shot.'

'I'm still listening, Monsieur Fumal.'

'I'm here as a friend, mind you.'

'So?'

'From the start, your attitude . . .'

'Has been polite, Monsieur Fumal.'

'Fine! Up to you. I asked to see you because I thought that, in light of our old friendship . . .'

They had never been friends, never played together. Besides, Ferdinand Fumal had never played with anyone, spending all his breaks alone in a corner.

'May I point out that I have a lot of work waiting for me?'

'I'm busier than you and I've still put myself out. I could have seen you in one of my offices . . .'

What was the point of arguing? It was true that this man knew the minister and had done him favours, as he probably had other politicians. This could end in trouble.

'Do you need the police?'

'Unofficially.'

'Go on.'

'It's understood that what I'm about to tell you is strictly between us.'

'Unless you've committed a crime . . .'

'I don't like jokes.'

His patience almost entirely exhausted, Maigret stood up and, fighting the urge to throw his visitor out, went and leaned on the mantelpiece.

'Someone wants to kill me.'

'I can see why,' Maigret almost said, but forced himself to remain impassive.

'For about a week I've been getting anonymous letters, which I barely took any notice of at first. If you're someone of my standing, you've got to expect you'll arouse jealousy in other people, sometimes even hatred.'

'Do you have the letters with you?'

Fumal took a wallet as bulging as his father's out of his pocket.

'Here's the first one. I threw away the envelope because I didn't know what was in it.'

Maigret took the letter and read in pencil:

You're dead.

Without smiling, he put the piece of paper on his desk.

'What do the others say?'

'This is the second, which came the next day. I kept the envelope, which, as you'll see, has the postmark of a post office near the Opéra.'

This time the note, which was also written in pencil, said in block capitals:

I'll have your guts.

There were others. Clutching the sheaf in his hand, Fumal handed them over one by one after first taking them out of their envelopes himself.

'I can't make out the postmark on this one.'

Count the days, bastard.

'I imagine you've no idea who sent them?'

'Wait. There's seven in all; the last one came this morning. One was posted on Boulevard Beaumarchais, another at the main post office on Rue du Louvre, and lastly one on Avenue des Ternes.'

The contents varied to a degree.

You haven't got long.
Make a will.
Scum.

Then the last one repeated the first:

You're dead.

'Are you leaving this correspondence in my care?'

Maigret had chosen the word 'correspondence' intentionally, slightly ironically.

'If it'll help you find out who sent them.'

'You don't think it's a practical joke?'

'Not many practical jokers in my world. Whatever you might think, Maigret, I'm not a person who scares easily. You don't get to where I am without making enemies, you see, and I've always despised mine.'

'So why are you here?'

'Because it's my right as a citizen to be protected. I don't want to be shot down without even knowing where the bullet's coming from. I talked it over with the minister, and he said . . .'

'I know. So, in a nutshell, you'd like us to provide you with some discreet security?'

'It seems appropriate.'

'And you'd probably also like us to find out who wrote these anonymous notes?'

'If you can.'

'Do you have anyone in particular in mind?'

'No, not in particular. Except . . .'

'Go on.'

'Mind you, I'm not accusing him. He's a weak man and, while he might be capable of threats, he wouldn't dare carry them out.'

'Who is it?'

'Someone called Gaillardin, Roger Gaillardin, from "Affordable Butchers".'

'Has he got any reason to hate you?'

'I've ruined him.'

'Intentionally?'

'Yes. After telling him I was going to.'

'Why?'

'Because he got in my way. His business is being wound up now, and I hope I'll get him sent to prison too, because on top of the bankruptcy there's been some trouble with cheques.'

'Do you have his address?'

'26, Rue François Premier.'

'Is he a butcher?'

'Not by profession. He's a money man. He handles other people's money. I handle my own. That's the whole difference between us.'

'Is he married?'

'Yes. But it's not his wife that matters. His mistress is the one. He lives with her.'

'Do you know her?'

'We've often gone out together, the three of us.'

'Are you married, Monsieur Fumal?'

'Have been for twenty-five years.'

'Did your wife come with you on these evenings out?'

'My wife hasn't been out for a long time.'

'Is she ill?'

'You could say that. At any rate she thinks so.'

'I'm going to take some notes.'

Maigret sat down, grabbed a folder and some paper.

'Your address?'

'I live in a private townhouse, which I own, at 58a, Boulevard de Courcelles, opposite Parc Monceau.'

'Nice part of town.'

'Yes. I have offices on Rue Rambuteau, near Les Halles, and also at La Villette.'

'I see.'

'Not to mention ones in Lille and elsewhere.'

'I imagine you have a large domestic staff.'

'Five servants at Boulevard de Courcelles.'

'Chauffeur?'

'I've never learned to drive.'

'Secretary?'

'I have a private secretary.'

'At Boulevard de Courcelles?'

'She has her bedroom and office there, but she comes with me when I go round the various branches.'

'Young?'

'I don't know. In her thirties, I suppose.'

'Are you sleeping with her?'

'No.'

'Who are you sleeping with?'

Fumal gave a contemptuous smile.

'I thought you'd ask me that. Well, yes, I do have a mistress. I've had several in fact. At the moment, it's someone called Martine Gilloux, whom I have set up in an apartment on Rue de l'Étoile.'

'Just around the corner.'

'Of course.'

'Where did you meet her?'

'In a nightclub, a year ago. She's a quiet sort and hardly ever goes out.'

'I don't suppose she has any reason to hate you?'

'I don't either.'

'Does she have a lover?'

'If she has, it's news to me,' he snapped. 'Anything else you want to know?'

'Yes. Is your wife jealous?'

'I suppose, with what I gather is your natural tact, you're going to ask her that yourself?'

'What sort of family is she from?'

'She's a butcher's daughter.'

'Perfect.'

'What's perfect?'

'Nothing. I'd like to get a better idea of the people close to you. Do you go through the post yourself?'

'I do with the post that comes to Boulevard de Courcelles.'

'Is that personal correspondence?'

'More or less. Everything else is sent to Rue Rambuteau and La Villette, where my office staff deals with it.'

'Your secretary doesn't . . .'

'She opens the envelopes and passes them to me.'

'Did you show her these notes?'

'No.'

'Why?'

'I don't know.'

'You didn't show your wife either?'

'No.'

'Your mistress?'

'Her neither. Are we finished?'

'I imagine I have your permission to go to Boulevard de Courcelles? What shall I say?'

'That I've lodged a complaint about some papers that have gone missing.'

'Can I go to your other offices as well?'

'Tell them the same.'

'And Rue de l'Étoile?'

'If you must.'

'Thank you.'

'Anything else?'

'I'm going to have your home guarded, starting this afternoon, but keeping track of your movements around Paris seems harder. I imagine you get about in a limousine?'

'Yes.'

'Are you armed?'

'I don't carry a gun on me but I've got a revolver in my bedside table.'

'Do you and your wife sleep in separate rooms?'

'Have done for ten years.'

Maigret had got to his feet and was looking at the door, then at his watch. Fumal laboriously stood up in his turn.

He cast around for something to say but could only come up with:

'I didn't expect this attitude from you.'

'Have I been rude?'

'I didn't say that, but . . .'

'I will take care of this matter, Monsieur Fumal. I hope nothing untoward happens to you.'

In the corridor, the meat tycoon retorted furiously:

'I hope not too. For your sake!'

Whereupon Maigret shut the door firmly.

2. *The Wary Secretary and the Deliberately Obtuse Wife*

Lucas came in holding some papers, trailing a smell of medicine, and Maigret, who hadn't gone back to his desk yet, gruffly asked:

'Did you see him?'

'Who, chief?'

'The guy who just went out.'

'We almost bumped into each other but I didn't really get a look at him.'

'That was a mistake. Unless I'm completely off the mark, he's going to cause us more trouble than the English-woman.'

Maigret had used a stronger word than 'trouble'. Besides irritation, he felt anxious now, weighed down. It worried him to see a kid whom he had always loathed and whose father had harmed his suddenly show up again from the distant past like this.

'Who was it?' asked Lucas, spreading his papers on the desk.

'Fumal.'

'As in meat?'

'Does that ring a bell?'

'My brother-in-law worked as an assistant accountant in one of his offices for a couple of years.'

'What does your brother-in-law think of him?'

'He didn't stay there for long.'

'Will you deal with it?'

Maigret pushed the threatening letters towards Lucas.

'Take them up to Moers first, just in case.'

It was rare that the lab technicians couldn't glean something from a document. Moers knew every make of paper, every type of ink and probably, when it came to it, every kind of pencil too. There was always a chance that they might also find some fingerprints that were already on file.

'How do we go about protecting him?' asked Lucas, after reading the threats.

'No idea. Start by sending someone to Boulevard de Courcelles. Vacher, say.'

'In the house or on the street?'

Maigret didn't answer immediately.

The rain had just stopped, but it wasn't an improvement. A cold, damp wind had got up which was forcing pedestrians to hold on to their hats and plastering their clothes against their bodies. A group walking across Pont Saint-Michel were leaning backwards as if they were being shoved in the chest.

'Outside. Get him to take someone with him to ask around the neighbourhood. You go and take a look at the offices on Rue Rambuteau and in La Villette.'

'Do you think the threats are genuine?'

'Fumal's is, at any rate. If we don't do what he wants, he'll set all his politician friends on us.'

'What does he want?'

'I've no idea.'

It was true. What did the meat wholesaler want exactly? What was the point of his visit?

'Are you going home for lunch?'

It was after twelve. For the past week, Maigret had been having lunch every other day in Place Dauphine, not for work reasons but because his wife had a dentist's appointment at 11.30. He didn't like eating on his own.

Lucas went with him. There were a few inspectors at the bar, as usual, and the two men went into the little back room, where a proper coal-fired stove of the sort Maigret loved had pride of place.

'How about a veal ragout?' suggested the restaurant owner.

'Perfect for me.'

A woman on the steps of the Palais de Justice was desperately trying to smooth down her dress, which a gust of wind had turned inside out like an umbrella.

After a moment, as the hors-d'oeuvres were being served, Maigret repeated, as if to himself, 'I don't understand . . .'

Maniacs or people who were mentally disturbed sometimes wrote letters like the ones Fumal had received. Occasionally they even carried out their threats. They were humble folk, generally people who had nursed a grievance for a long time without daring to give any hint of it.

A man like Fumal must have wronged hundreds of individuals. His arrogance would have hurt others.

What Maigret didn't understand was the nature of his visit, the aggressive way he had behaved.

Had Maigret started it? Had he been wrong to show he still felt a grudge that dated back to the village of Saint-Fiacre?

'Hasn't the Yard rung you today, chief?'

'Not yet. They will.'

A veal ragout of a creaminess even Madame Maigret couldn't have improved on was brought to the table. Moments later the restaurant owner appeared to say that Maigret was wanted on the telephone. Only people at headquarters knew where to find him.

'Yes. Go ahead . . . Janin? What does she want? Ask her to wait a moment . . . You know, about a quarter of an hour . . . Yes . . . In the waiting room, that's better . . .'

When he went back to his seat, he told Lucas:

'His secretary is asking to talk to me. She's at headquarters.'

'Did she know her boss was meant to pay you a visit?'

Maigret shrugged and started eating. He didn't have any cheese or fruit, just a black coffee, which he drank boiling hot as he filled his pipe.

'Don't rush. Do what I told you to and keep me posted.'

He was definitely starting a cold himself. Under the archway of the Police Judiciaire the wind whipped off his hat, and the policeman on duty only just caught it.

'Thanks, my friend.'

On the first floor, he looked curiously through the windows of the waiting room at a young woman in her thirties. Blonde, with regular features, she was waiting with both hands propped on her handbag, showing no sign of impatience.

'Did you want to talk to me?'

'Detective Chief Inspector Maigret?'

'Follow me . . . Take a seat . . .'

He took off his overcoat and hat and sat down in his chair, then looked at her again. Without waiting to be asked anything, she began confidently, her voice settling almost immediately into its natural tone:

'My name is Louise Bourges and I am Monsieur Fumal's personal secretary.'

'Have you worked for him for a long time?'

'Three years.'

'I understand that you live on Boulevard de Courcelles, in your employer's townhouse?'

'Generally speaking, yes. But I still have a little apartment on Quai Voltaire.'

'Go on.'

'Monsieur Fumal will have been to see you this morning.'

'Did he tell you about it?'

'No. I heard him on the telephone to the minister of the interior.'

'While you were in the room?'

'I wouldn't have known otherwise; I don't listen at doors.'

'Is that visit what you want to talk to me about?'

She nodded but took her time answering, searching for the right words.

'Monsieur Fumal doesn't know I'm here.'

'Where is he now?'

'In an expensive restaurant on the Left Bank, where he

has invited several people for lunch. He has business lunches almost every day.'

Maigret wasn't helping her, or discouraging her either. To tell the truth, he was wondering as he looked at her why, despite a well-proportioned, shapely figure and regular, rather pretty features, she wasn't more attractive.

'I don't want to waste your time, inspector. I'm not sure exactly what Monsieur Fumal told you. I'm assuming he brought you some letters.'

'Have you read them?'

'The first one, and at least one other. The first because I was the one who opened it, the other because he left it lying on his desk.'

'How do you know that there are more than two?'

'Because I handle all the post and I recognized the block capitals as well as the yellowish paper of the envelopes.'

'Has Monsieur Fumal talked to you about them?'

'No.'

She hesitated again, although without becoming flustered, despite Maigret's insistent stare.

'I think you should know that he wrote them.'

Her cheeks had become pinker, and she seemed relieved now she had managed to spit it out.

'What makes you think that?'

'I caught him writing them once, for a start. I never knock before going into his office – it's his idea. He thought I'd gone out, but in fact I'd forgotten something. I went back into the office and saw him writing in block capitals on a sheet of paper.'

'What day was that?'

'The day before yesterday.'

'Did he seem annoyed?'

'He immediately put a blotter over the piece of paper. Yesterday I wondered where he'd got the paper and the envelopes. We don't have any like it at Boulevard de Cour-celles or in the Rue Rambuteau offices, or anywhere else. As you'll have seen, it's the sort of cheap paper they sell in grocers' and tobacconists' in packs. When he was away I started looking.'

'Did you come up with anything?'

She opened her bag and took out a sheet of lined paper and a yellowish envelope, which she handed to him.

'Where did you get these?'

'In a cabinet full of old files we don't use any more.'

'May I ask, mademoiselle, why you decided to come and see me?'

She started, but only slightly, and immediately recov-ered her poise. In a clear voice, with a touch of defiance, she replied:

'To protect myself.'

'Against what?'

'Against him.'

'I don't understand.'

'Because you don't know him the way I do.'

She didn't suspect that Maigret had known him much longer than she had.

'Explain.'

'There's nothing to explain. He never does anything without a reason, you understand? If he goes to the trou-ble of sending himself threatening letters, he's up to something. Especially if he then disturbs the minister of the interior and comes to see you.'

Her reasoning couldn't be faulted.

'Do you think, inspector, that there are fundamentally wicked people, I mean wicked for the sake of it?'

Maigret preferred not to answer.

'Well, that's what he's like. He employs, directly or indirectly, hundreds of people and he does everything in his power to make their lives as miserable as possible. He's sly too. It's almost impossible to hide anything from him. His managers, who are badly paid, all try to cheat him in different ways, and he loves catching them out when they least expect it.

'There was an old cashier at Rue Rambuteau whom he loathed for absolutely no reason but still kept on for almost thirty years because he did odd jobs for him. He was like a sort of slave; he started shaking whenever his master was near. He was poorly, had six or seven children.

'When his health deteriorated, Monsieur Fumal decided to get rid of him without paying him any compensation, or even acknowledging his debt of gratitude. Do you know what he did?

'He went to Rue Rambuteau one night and took some cash out of the safe, which only he and the cashier had keys to.

'Then the next morning in the office he slipped some of the money into the cashier's sports jacket, which the man used to hang on a nail when he got to work so he could change into an old coat.

'Then he had the safe opened on some pretext or other.

You can guess the rest. The veteran employee wept like a child, went down on his knees. Apparently it was horrendous. Monsieur Fumal threatened to call the police until the very last minute, so that in the end it was the poor man who left saying thank you.

'Do you understand now why I wanted to protect myself?'

He muttered distractedly:

'I do.'

'I've only given you one example. There's more. He never does anything without an ulterior motive and his motives are always unpredictable.'

'Do you think he fears for his life?'

'I'm sure he does. He's always been afraid. In fact that's why, strange though it may seem, he told me not to knock on his door. Hearing a sudden knock at the door makes him jump.'

'So, in your opinion there are a certain number of people who have good reason to resent him?'

'Plenty, yes.'

'Everyone who works for him, essentially?'

'As well as the people he does business with. He has ruined dozens of small butchers who've refused to sell up. Monsieur Gaillardin was the most recent.'

'Do you know him?'

'Yes.'

'What's he like?'

'A very nice man. He lives in a beautiful apartment on Rue François Premier with a mistress twenty years younger than him. He had a good business and lived a comfortable life until the day Monsieur Fumal decided to set up Associated Butchers. It's a long story. They fought for two years, and in the end Monsieur Gaillardin had to beg for mercy.'

'Don't you like your employer?'

'No, inspector.'

'Why do you keep working for him?'

She blushed for the second time but again wasn't thrown.

'Because of Félix.'

'Who is Félix?'

'The chauffeur.'

'Are you the chauffeur's lover?'

'If you want to be crude, yes. We're engaged too, and we're going to get married when we've put aside enough money to buy an inn near Gien.'

'Why Gien?'

'Because we're both from there.'

'Did you know each other before you came to Paris?'

'No. We met at Boulevard de Courcelles.'

'Does Monsieur Fumal know about your plans?'

'I hope not.'

'And your relationship?'

'Knowing him as I do, he probably does know about that. He's not the sort of person you can hide things from. I'm sure he spies on us now and again. He's careful not to let it slip, though. He only comes out with things when there's something in it for him.'

'I imagine Félix feels the same way about him as you do?'

'Absolutely.'

The young woman couldn't be accused of a lack of frankness.

'There's a Madame Fumal, isn't there?'

'Yes. They got married a long time ago.'

'What is she like?'

'What do you expect her to be like with a husband like him? He terrorizes her.'

'What do you mean?'

'She's like a shadow in that house. He comes and goes, swans in and out, brings home friends and business acquaintances. He pays her no more mind than a servant, never takes her to a restaurant and in the summer packs her off to spend her holidays in a little backwater in the mountains.'

'Was she a beauty?'

'No. Her father was one of the biggest butchers in Paris, on Rue du Faubourg Saint-Honoré, and in those days Monsieur Fumal wasn't rich yet.'

'Do you think she's suffering?'

'I wouldn't even say that. She doesn't care about anything. She sleeps, drinks, reads novels and sometimes goes to the nearest cinema on her own.'

'Is she younger than him?'

'Probably. You couldn't tell, though.'

'Is there anything else you want to tell me?'

'I'd better be going so I can be back by the time he gets to Boulevard de Courcelles.'

'Do you have your meals there?'

'Usually.'

'With the staff?'

She nodded, and for the third time her cheeks reddened.

'Thank you, mademoiselle. I'll probably drop by this afternoon.'

'You won't tell him . . .'

'Don't worry.'

'He's so sly . . .'

'So am I!'

He watched her walk off down the long corridor, start down the stairs and then disappear from sight.

Why on earth was Ferdinand Fumal sending himself threatening letters and asking for police protection? An answer immediately came to mind, but Maigret didn't like overly simple explanations.

This one went: Fumal had plenty of enemies, some of whom resented him enough to make an attempt on his life. Who knew if he hadn't recently given someone even greater cause to hate him?

He couldn't go to the police and say:

'I'm a bastard. One of my victims could be planning to kill me. Protect me.'

So he went about it in a roundabout way, sending himself anonymous letters, which he then waved in Maigret's face.

Was that it? Or was it more likely that Mademoiselle Bourges had been lying?

Unable to make up his mind, Maigret started up the staircase leading to the laboratory. Moers was working, and he handed him the sheet of paper and envelope the secretary had just given him.

'Have you found anything?'

'Fingerprints.'

'Whose?'

'Three people's. A man's first, I don't know who, with wide, square fingers, then yours and Lucas'.'

'Anything else?'

'No.'

'Are this piece of paper and envelope the same as the others?'

Moers didn't need to examine them for long to be certain they were.

'Naturally I haven't dusted the envelopes for prints. There's always lots of different ones, including the postman's.'

When Maigret got back to his office he was tempted to forget about Fumal and his story. How are you supposed to protect a man who drives all over Paris without putting at least a dozen officers on the job?

'Rotten bastard!' he muttered a few times through gritted teeth.

Someone rang about Mrs Britt. Another lead which they'd been following for a day, which turned out to be a dead end.

'If anyone asks for me,' he announced, going into the inspectors' office, 'I'll be back in an hour or two.'

Downstairs he chose one of the black cars.

'Boulevard de Courcelles. 58a.'

It had started to rain again. You could tell from the expressions on the faces of passers-by that they were sick of splashing through the cold rain and mud.

Built around the end of the last century, the townhouse was palatial, with a carriage entrance, bars on the ground-floor windows and very tall windows on the first floor. He pressed a brass doorbell. Eventually a manservant in a striped waistcoat opened the door.

'Monsieur Fumal, please.'

'He's not here.'

'In that case I'll see Madame Fumal.'

'I don't know if Madame can see you.'

'Tell her it's Detective Chief Inspector Maigret.'

At the far end of the courtyard a row of what had once been stables was used as garages, and he could see two cars, which suggested the former butcher had at least three.

'If you'd care to follow me . . .'

A broad staircase with a carved bannister led up to a first-floor landing flanked by two marble statues that looked as if they were standing guard. Maigret was asked to wait and took a seat on an uncomfortable Renaissance chair.

The manservant continued upstairs and was gone for a long time. Whisperings could be heard on the floor above, as well as the click-click of a typewriter some-where: Mademoiselle Bourges at work, probably.

'Madame will see you in a moment. If you'd be so kind as to continue waiting . . .'

The manservant went back down to the ground floor, and almost a quarter of an hour passed before a maid came down from the second floor.

'Detective Chief Inspector Maigret? This way please . . .'

The house was as gloomy as a magistrate's court. There was too much space and not enough life; voices echoed off the imitation-marble walls.

Maigret was shown into an old-fashioned drawing room with a grand piano surrounded by at least fifteen armchairs upholstered in faded tapestry. He waited a little longer. Finally, the door opened to admit a woman in a housecoat whose expressionless eyes, puffy, pale face and inky black hair reminded him of an apparition.

'I'm sorry to keep you waiting . . .'

Her voice was flat, like a sleepwalker's.

'Sit down, please. Are you sure you want to see me?'

Louise Bourges had hinted at the truth when she spoke about her drinking, but the reality was far worse than Maigret had imagined. The woman opposite him wore a weary but resigned expression, devoid of emotion, and seemed in a different world.

'Your husband came to see me this morning. He has reason to believe that someone wants to kill him.'

She didn't recoil, just looked at him with the vaguest hint of surprise.

'Did he tell you?'

'He doesn't tell me anything.'

'Do you know if he has any enemies?'

The words seemed to take a long time to reach her brain, then time was also needed for an answer to take shape.

'I suppose he has, don't you?' she muttered eventually.

'Did you marry for love?'

This was too much for her to understand. Her only response was:

'I don't know.'

'Do you have children, Madame Fumal?'

She shook her head.

'Would your husband have liked children?'

She repeated:

'I don't know.'

Then she added, indifferently:

'I suppose so.'

What else could he ask her? It seemed almost impossible to communicate with her, as if she lived in a different world or as if they were separated by the impenetrable walls of a glass cage.

'I imagine I've interrupted your afternoon nap?'

'No. I don't take a nap.'

'Well, all that remains . . .'

Well, all that remained was for him to leave, and that's what he was about to do when the door was shoved open.

'What on earth are you doing in here?' asked Fumal, with a harder look than ever.

'As you can see, I'm introducing myself to your wife.'

'First they tell me one of your men is downstairs questioning my staff. Now I find you in here tormenting my wife, who . . .'

'One moment, Monsieur Fumal. You were the one who came to me for help, weren't you?'

'I didn't give you permission to interfere in my private life.'

Maigret waved goodbye to the woman, who was looking at them uncomprehendingly.

'I'm sorry, madame. I hope I haven't disturbed you too much.'

The master of the house followed him out on to the landing.

'What did you talk to her about?'

'I asked her if she knew of any enemies you might have.'

'What did she say?'

'That you must have some but that she didn't know who they were.'

'Does that get you anywhere?'

'No.'

'Well?'

'Well nothing.'

Maigret almost asked him why he had sent himself anonymous letters but thought it wasn't the moment.

'Is there anyone else in the house you'd like to question?'

'One of my inspectors is seeing to it. He's downstairs, as I now know, thanks to you. Incidentally, if you really are serious about being protected, it might be better to let one of our men accompany you when you're out and about. It's all very well watching the house, but when you're over at Rue Rambuteau or anywhere else . . .'

They were both on the stairs. Fumal appeared to be thinking, scrutinizing Maigret as if he was wondering whether a trap was being set for him.

'Starting when?'

'Whenever you like.'

'Tomorrow morning?'

'Fine. I'll send someone tomorrow morning. When do you usually leave the house?'

'It depends on the day. Tomorrow I'm going to La Villette at eight.'

'An inspector will be here at seven thirty.'

They had heard the carriage entrance open and close. When they got to the first floor, they saw a short, bald man coming towards them, dressed entirely in black, carrying his hat in his hand. He seemed very at home and looked inquiringly first at Maigret, then at Fumal.

'This is Detective Chief Inspector Maigret, Joseph,' Fumal said. 'There was a small matter I had to attend to with him.'

Then, turning to Maigret, he went on:

'Joseph Goldman, my business manager – my right hand, I should say. Everyone calls him Monsieur Joseph.'

Monsieur Joseph had a black leather briefcase under his arm. He gave a strange smile, revealing a row of bad teeth.

'I won't see you to the door, inspector. Victor will show you out.'

Victor, the manservant in the striped waistcoat, was waiting at the bottom of the stairs.

'So, we're agreed about tomorrow morning.'

'All agreed,' repeated Maigret.

He didn't remember ever having such a feeling of powerlessness, or, more precisely, unreality. Even the building seemed fake! He sensed the manservant give a mocking smile as he closed the door behind him.

When he got back to headquarters he debated who to send the next day to watch over Fumal and ended up choosing Lapointe. He briefed him:

'Be there by seven thirty. Go with him wherever he goes. He'll take you in his car. He'll probably try to needle you.'

'Why?'

'Doesn't matter. Don't rise to the bait.'

As for him, he had to attend to the old Englishwoman, who reports were now claiming had travelled to Maubeuge. It could easily not be her. They'd given up counting the false leads they'd investigated, the number of old Englishwomen sighted all over France.

Vacher rang to ask for instructions.

'What shall I do? Keep watch inside or outside the house?'

'Whichever you like.'

'Even with the rain, I'd rather be outside.'

Someone else who didn't like the atmosphere in the Boulevard de Courcelles mansion.

'I'll have you relieved around midnight.'

'OK, chief. Thanks.'

Maigret had supper at home. That night his wife wasn't in pain, and he slept straight through to 7.30. As always she brought him a cup of coffee in bed, and his eyes turned immediately to the window. The sky was as leaden as ever.

He had just gone into the bathroom when the telephone rang. He heard his wife answering:

'Yes . . . yes . . . One moment, Monsieur Lapointe.'

That was bad. At 7.30, Lapointe would be starting his shift at Boulevard de Courcelles. If he was ringing . . .

'Hello . . . It's me . . .'

'Listen, chief . . . Something's happened . . .'

'Dead?'

'Yes.'

'How?'

'We don't know. Maybe poisoned. There's no visible wound. I didn't really take time to look. The doctor hasn't arrived yet.'

'I'm on my way!'

Had he been so wrong in thinking that Fumal was going to be a pain in the . . . trouble through and through?

3. The Manservant's Past and the Tenant on the Third Floor

Maigret felt a pang of guilt as he shaved – perhaps because he'd had a grudge against Fumal. It made him wonder if he had done his job thoroughly. The meat wholesaler had come to him to ask for his protection. He had done so aggressively, admittedly, getting the minister to pull strings and using barely veiled threats. But Maigret still had to do his duty. Had he done so as fully as possible? He had gone to Boulevard de Courcelles in person, but he hadn't taken the trouble to check all the doors and exits. He had put off that chore until the next day, along with the task of interviewing all the staff in turn.

He had posted an inspector in front of the house. From 7.30 this morning, if Fumal hadn't been killed, Lapointe would have been guarding him while Lucas pursued his investigations in Rue Rambuteau and elsewhere.

Would he have acted differently if he hadn't disliked the man, if he hadn't had an old score to settle with him, if it had just been any big businessman in Paris?

Before he had breakfast, he telephoned the prosecutor, then Quai des Orfèvres.

'Aren't they sending a car?' asked Madame Maigret, who took up as little space as possible at moments like this.

'I'll take a taxi.'

The boulevards were almost empty, with just a few dark silhouettes emerging from the Métro and hurrying towards the townhouses. A car – a doctor's – was parked opposite 58a, Boulevard de Courcelles, and when Maigret rang the bell, the door opened immediately.

The manservant from the previous day hadn't had time to shave, but he was already wearing his yellow and black striped waistcoat. He had very bushy eyebrows, and Maigret studied him for a moment as if he was trying to remember something.

'Where to?' he asked.

'First floor, the office.'

As he climbed the stairs, he resolved to look into this Victor later; he intrigued him. Lapointe came to meet him on the landing, which was doubling as a waiting room.

'I made a mistake, chief, sorry. The way he was lying when I saw him, you couldn't see the wound.'

'He wasn't poisoned?'

'No. When he turned him over, the doctor found a massive wound in his back, level with the heart. The shot was fired point-blank.'

'Where's his wife?'

'I don't know. She hasn't come downstairs.'

'The secretary?'

'She must be through there. Come with me. I'm only just getting the hang of this place.'

At the front of the house, overlooking the railings of Parc Monceau, there was an enormous drawing room that gave the impression of never being used. It was damp despite the central heating.

Along a red-carpeted corridor they found a first, relatively small office on the right, looking on to the courtyard. Louise Bourges was in there, standing by the window, and a maid was with her. Neither of them said anything. Louise Bourges looked at Maigret anxiously, no doubt wondering how he was going to treat her after her visit the previous day to Quai des Orfèvres.

'Where is he?' he simply asked.

She pointed to a door.

'In there.'

It was another office, more spacious, also red-carpeted and with Empire-style furniture. A human form was stretched out on the floor by an armchair, with a doctor whom Maigret didn't know on his knees by it.

'I'm told it was a gunshot fired at point-blank range, is that right?'

The doctor nodded. Maigret had already noticed that the dead man hadn't changed for bed and was still wearing the same clothes as the day before.

'What time did it happen?'

'As far as I can tell at first sight, towards the end of the evening, between eleven and midnight, say.'

Involuntarily Maigret thought of the village of Saint-Fiacre, the school yard, the fat boy no one liked whom they called Boom-Boom or Gumdrop.

Turning him over, the doctor had put him into a strange pose. An outstretched arm seemed to be pointing to a corner of the room, which was empty except for a yellow marble nymph on a plinth.

'I suppose death was instantaneous?'

This was a pointless question – the wound was almost big enough to fit a fist in – but Maigret wasn't his usual self. This didn't feel like an ordinary case.

'Does his wife know?'

'I think so.'

He went into the next room, repeated the question to the secretary:

'Does his wife know?'

'Yes. Noémi went up to tell her.'

'Hasn't she come down?'

He was starting to realize that nothing happened here as it would in a normal household.

'When did you last see him?'

'Yesterday evening, around nine o'clock.'

'Did he send for you?'

'Yes.'

'Why?'

'To dictate some letters. The shorthand is on my pad. I haven't typed them up yet.'

'Important letters?'

'Not especially. He often made me take dictation in the evening.'

Maigret understood what the young woman was thinking: her employer made a point of calling her back after a day's work to needle her. Ferdinand Fumal had spent his whole life needling people?

'Did he have any visitors?'

'Not while I was there.'

'Was he expecting any?'

'I think so. He received a telephone call and told me to go to bed.'

'What time was that?'

'Nine thirty.'

'Did you go to bed?'

'Yes.'

'Alone?'

'No.'

'Where is your bedroom?'

'With the other staff bedrooms, above the old stables which are now garages.'

'Were Monsieur Fumal and his wife the only people who slept in the house?'

'No. Victor sleeps on the ground floor.'

'Is that the manservant?'

'He's also the concierge and the caretaker and he does the shopping.'

'Isn't he married?'

'No. At least not that I know of. He has a little room with an ox-eye window under the archway.'

'Thank you.'

'What should I do?'

'Wait. When the post arrives, bring it to me. I wonder if there'll be another anonymous letter.'

He sensed she was blushing but wasn't sure. Footsteps could be heard on the stairs. The deputy public prosecutor was accompanied by a young examining magistrate called Planche, with whom Maigret hadn't had the chance to work yet. The court clerk who followed them had a cold. Almost immediately after they arrived, the carriage entrance opened again to admit the people from Criminal Records.

Louise Bourges was still standing by the window in her office, awaiting instructions. After a moment Maigret spoke to her again.

'Who told Madame Fumal?'

'Noémi.'

'Is that her personal maid?'

'She does the second floor. Monsieur Fumal's bedroom is on that floor, next to his office.'

'Go and see what's happening up there.'

She hesitated, and he asked:

'What are you afraid of?'

'Nothing.'

It was odd, to say the least, that the dead man's wife hadn't come downstairs yet and that there wasn't a sound to be heard on her floor.

Since Maigret had got there, Lapointe had been silently rummaging about all over the house looking for a gun. He had opened the door of the vast master bedroom, which was also decorated in Empire style, with a pair of pyjamas and a dressing gown laid out on the turned-down bed.

Even with its tall windows, the mansion was murky and grey, and only a few lights had been switched on. Here and there police photographers were setting up their equipment, while the prosecutor's people whispered in a corner as they waited for the forensics doctor to arrive.

'Any ideas, Maigret?'

'None.'

'Did you know him?'

'I knew him at my village school and he came to see me yesterday. He went to the minister of the interior to ask for our protection.'

'Against what?'

'He had been receiving anonymous threats for a time.'

'Didn't you do anything?'

'One of my men spent the night on his doorstep and another was going to take over during the day.'

'Well, anyway, it looks as if the killer took his gun with him.'

Lapointe hadn't found anything. Nor had anyone else. Maigret set off downstairs with his hands in his pockets. Reaching the ground floor, he pressed his face to the ox-eye window he had been told about.

There was a room in there that looked like a concierge's lodge, with a messy bed, a mirrored wardrobe, a gas stove, a table, some books on a shelf. The manservant was sitting astride a chair, his elbows propped on the back of it, staring blankly into space.

Maigret rapped on the window a few times before the man started and looked at him, blinking, then stood up and came to the door.

'Recognized me yet?' he asked, a fearful, wary look on his face.

Maigret had had a sense the day before that he'd seen him somewhere, but he still hadn't worked out where.

'I recognized you immediately.'

'Who are you?'

'You didn't know me back then because I'm a good bit younger than you. You'd already left when I was born.'

'Left where?'

'Saint-Fiacre, of course! Don't you remember Nicolas?'

Maigret remembered him all too well. He was an old drunk who did the odd day's agricultural labour, worked on the threshing machine in the summer and rang the bells in church on a Sunday. He lived in a hut on the edge of the woods and was known to eat crows and polecats.

'He was my father.'

'Is he dead?'

'Has been for a long time.'

'What about you – how long have you been in Paris?'

'Didn't you see anything about it in the papers? They even used my picture. I had some trouble back there. In the end, they realized I hadn't done it on purpose.'

He had bushy hair and a low forehead.

'Tell me what happened.'

'I was out poaching – no two ways about it, I've never tried to deny it.'

'And you killed a gamekeeper?'

'Did you read about it?'

'Who was it?'

'A young one, you didn't know him. He was always after me. I swear, I didn't do it on purpose. I was watching for a deer and when I heard a noise in the undergrowth . . .'

'What gave you the idea of coming here after that?'

'It wasn't my idea.'

'Fumal came and got you?'

'Yes. He needed someone he could trust. You've never

48

been back to the village, have you – not that you've been forgotten there; they're proud of you, I can tell you – but as soon as he had the money, he bought Saint-Fiacre chateau . . .'

Maigret felt sick at heart. He had been born there. Only on the estate, it's true, but it was still his birthplace, and for a long time the countess of Saint-Fiacre had been his ideal of womanhood.

'I get the picture,' he muttered.

Fumal surrounded himself with people he had a hold over – that was it, wasn't it? He needed some sort of body-guard, or bulldog, more than a manservant so he brought a strapping lad back to Paris who had escaped hard labour by the skin of his teeth.

'Did he pay for your lawyer?'

'How do you know that?'

'Tell me what happened yesterday evening.'

'Nothing happened. Monsieur didn't go out.'

'What time did he get back?'

'Just before eight, for dinner.'

'Alone?'

'With Mademoiselle Louise.'

'Was the car put away in the garage?'

'Yes. It's still there. All three are.'

'Does the secretary eat with the servants?'

'She likes to, because of Félix.'

'Does everyone know about her relationship with Félix?'

'It's pretty obvious.'

'Did your boss know too?'

Victor was silent. Maigret said:

'You told him, didn't you?'

'Yes.'

'If I understand correctly, you told him everything that was happening in the servants' quarters?'

'He paid me to.'

'Let's get back to yesterday evening. Did you leave your lodge?'

'No. Germaine brought me my dinner here.'

'Did that happen every evening?'

'Yes.'

'Which one is Germaine?'

'The oldest.'

'Did anyone come to the door?'

'Monsieur Joseph got back around nine thirty.'

'You mean he lives in the house?'

'Didn't you know?'

Maigret hadn't suspected it for a moment.

'Give me details. Where's his bedroom?'

'It isn't a bedroom, it's a whole apartment on the third floor. They're attic rooms with sloping ceilings, but they're bigger than the ones over the garage. They were the maids' rooms before.'

'How long has he lived in the house?'

'I don't know. Before my time.'

'How long have you been here?'

'Five years.'

'Where does Monsieur Joseph have his meals?'

'Mostly at a brasserie on Boulevard des Batignolles.'

'Is he a bachelor?'

'A widower, from what I've heard.'

'Is he ever gone for the night?'

'No, except when he's travelling, of course.'

'Does he travel a lot?'

'He goes to the country branches to check the books.'

'What time did you say he got back?'

'About nine thirty.'

'Did he go out again?'

'No.'

'Did anyone else come to the house?'

'Monsieur Gaillardin.'

'How do you know him?'

'I've let him in lots of times. He used to be a good friend of the boss. Then they fell out, and yesterday was the first time in a long while that . . .'

'Did you send him upstairs?'

'Monsieur rang telling me to show him up. There's an internal telephone from the office to my lodge.'

'What time was that?'

'Around ten o'clock. You know, I always used to tell the time by the sun, so it doesn't often occur to me to look at the clock. Especially because the one in here is always at least ten minutes fast.'

'How long was he upstairs?'

'Maybe a quarter of an hour.'

'How did you open the door for him when he left?'

'By pressing the switch here, same as in any concierge's lodge.'

'Did you see him go past?'

'Of course.'

'Did you have a look at him?'

'Well . . .'

He hesitated, his anxiety returning.

'That depends on what you call have a look. There isn't much light under the archway. I didn't press my face to the window. I just saw him, you know. I recognized him. I'm sure it was him.'

'But you don't know what mood he was in?'

'No clue.'

'Did your boss call you after that?'

'Why?'

'Answer the question.'

'No . . . I don't think so . . . Wait . . . No . . . I went to bed. I read some of the paper in bed, then I turned out the light.'

'Which means that no one came into the house after Gaillardin left?'

Victor started to speak, then changed his mind.

'Isn't that correct?' insisted Maigret.

'It's correct, yes, of course . . . But it might also not be . . . It's not easy summing up people's lives just like that, in a few minutes . . . I don't even know what you know . . .'

'What do you mean?'

'What did they tell you upstairs?'

'Who?'

'Oh, well, Mademoiselle Louise or Noémi or Germaine . . .'

'Could someone have come in last night without you knowing?'

'Definitely!'

'Who?'

'The boss, for a start. He could have gone out and come back in. Haven't you seen the little door on Rue de Prony? It used to be the servants' entrance and he's got the key.'

'Does he use it sometimes?'

'I don't think so. I don't know.'

'Who else has a key?'

'Monsieur Joseph. I'm sure about that, because I once saw him going out in the morning when I hadn't seen him come back in the night before.'

'Who else?'

'Probably the fancy woman.'

'Who do you mean by that?'

'The boss's fancy woman, the latest one, a little brunette, don't know her name, who lives around l'Étoile.'

'Was she here last night?'

'I'll say it again, I haven't got a clue. I've had this happen to me once before, you see, with the gamekeeper. The questioning went on so long they made me make up things. They even made me sign a statement saying it was all true, and then later they used it against me.'

'Did you like your boss?'

'What difference does that make?'

'Aren't you going to answer?'

'All I'll say is that it's got nothing to do with anything, and it's nobody's business but mine.'

'As you wish.'

'The only reason I'm talking to you in the first place . . .'

'I understand.'

It was better not to insist, and Maigret slowly went back up to the first floor.

'Hasn't Madame Fumal come down yet?' he asked the secretary.

'She doesn't want to see him until he's been tidied up.'

'How is she?'

'Same as always.'

'Didn't she seem surprised?'

Louise Bourges shrugged. She was more on edge than the day before, and Maigret saw her biting her nails several times.

'I can't find a gun, chief. They're asking if they can take the body to the Forensic Institute.'

'What does the examining magistrate say?'

'He's happy for them to.'

'Then so am I.'

Victor brought up the post just then. He turned to Louise Bourges, then hesitated.

'Over here!' said Maigret.

There were fewer letters than he would have imagined. Presumably most of Fumal's post went to his various offices. Here it was mainly bills, a couple of invitations to charity events, a letter from a lawyer in Nevers and finally an envelope that Maigret recognized immediately. Louise Bourges was watching him intently from across the room.

The address was written in pencil. On a sheet of cheap paper only two words were written:

Final warning.

Wasn't this becoming almost ironic?

At that moment Ferdinand Fumal, lying on a stretcher,

was leaving his townhouse on Boulevard de Courcelles, just opposite the main entrance of Parc Monceau with its dripping trees.

'Look up Gaillardin, Rue François Premier, in the phonebook for me.'

The secretary passed Lapointe the telephone directory.

'Roger?' he asked.

'Yes. Get him on the telephone.'

It wasn't a man who answered the inspector's call.

'I'm sorry to disturb you, madame. I'd like to speak to Monsieur Gaillardin . . . Yes . . . What's that? He's not at home?'

Lapointe looked inquiringly at Maigret.

'It's very urgent . . . Do you know if he's at the office? You don't know? You think he's travelling? One moment . . . Stay on the line . . .'

'Ask her if he spent last night at Rue François Premier.'

'Hello. Can you tell me if Monsieur Gaillardin spent last night at home? No . . . When did you see him last? You had dinner together? At Fouquet's? And he left you at . . . I can't hear . . . Just before nine thirty . . . Without telling you where he was going . . . I understand . . . Yes . . . Thank you . . . No, there's no message . . .'

He explained to Maigret:

'From what I understand, she's his mistress, not his wife, and he doesn't seem to be in the habit of explaining himself to her.'

Two inspectors, who had arrived some time ago, were giving the Criminal Records' people a hand.

'Hey, Neveu, get over to Rue François Premier as quick

as you can . . . The address is in the book . . . Gaillardin . . . Try and find out if he took any luggage, if he seemed to be planning on leaving, anything like that . . . Make sure you get a photograph . . . And circulate his description to the stations and airports, just to be on the safe side . . .'

It all seemed too easy. Maigret didn't dare get his hopes up.

'Did you know,' he asked Louise Bourges, 'that Gaillardin was meant to be coming over yesterday evening to see your employer?'

'As I said, I know that someone telephoned and he answered something like: "Fine."'

'What mood was he in?'

'His usual.'

'Was Monsieur Joseph in and out of his office during the evening?'

'I think so.'

'Where is Monsieur Joseph at the moment?'

'Upstairs probably.'

He may have been upstairs a short while ago but he wasn't now because they saw him cross the landing, looking around in amazement.

It was a shock after the frenetic activity that had thrown the house into turmoil to see the greyish little man emerge from the stairs as if nothing was amiss and ask in an artless voice:

'What's happening?'

'Didn't you hear anything?' Maigret asked gruffly.

'Hear what? Where's Monsieur Fumal?'

'He's dead.'

'What did you say?'

'I said that he's dead, and his body has already been moved out of the house. Are you a deep sleeper, Monsieur Joseph?'

'I sleep like anyone else.'

'Haven't you heard anything since seven thirty this morning?'

'I heard someone going into Madame Fumal's room on the floor below mine.'

'What time did you go to bed last night?'

'Around ten thirty.'

'When did you leave your employer?'

The little man still didn't seem to understand what was happening to him.

'Why are you asking me these questions?'

'Because Fumal has been murdered. Did you go down to see him yesterday after dinner?'

'No, but I stopped in to see him when I got back.'

'What time?'

'Around nine thirty. A little after, maybe.'

'And then?'

'Then nothing. I went up to my apartment, worked for an hour and went to bed.'

'Did you hear a gunshot?'

'You can't hear anything on this floor from upstairs.'

'Do you have a revolver?'

'Me? I've never touched a gun in my life. I didn't even do my military service, I failed the medical.'

'Did you know that Fumal had one?'

'He showed it to me.'

Under some papers in the drawer of the bedside table they had finally found a Belgian-made automatic. It hadn't been fired for years, so couldn't have had anything to do with the crime.

'Did you also know that Fumal was expecting a visit?'

No one gave immediate answers in this house. After every question there was a pause, as if they had to repeat the question to themselves a few times before they could understand it.

'From who?'

'Don't play dumb, Monsieur Joseph. Incidentally, what is your full name?'

'Joseph Goldman. You were told it yesterday when we were introduced.'

'What was your profession before you started working for Fumal?'

'I was a bailiff for twenty-two years. And it's not quite right to say I was working for him. That makes me sound like a servant or an employee. In fact I was a friend, an advisor.'

'You mean you devoted all your energies to making his crooked schemes vaguely legal?'

'Careful, inspector. There are witnesses.'

'So?'

'I could hold you accountable for your rash language.'

'What do you know about Gaillardin's visit?'

The little old man pursed his strikingly thin lips.

'Nothing.'

'I suppose you don't know anything either about

someone called Martine, who lives in Rue de l'Étoile and probably has a key to the small door like you?'

'I never have anything to do with the women.'

Maigret had barely been in the house for an hour and a half and he already felt he was suffocating. He couldn't wait to get out and breathe fresh air, however damp.

'Please stay here.'

'Can't I go to Rue Rambuteau? I'm expected there to make some important decisions. You seem to be losing sight of the fact that we are responsible for Paris' meat supply, or an eighth of it at least, and . . .'

'One of my inspectors will go with you.'

'Meaning?'

'Nothing, Monsieur Joseph. Nothing whatsoever!'

Maigret was on edge. The prosecutor's men were taking the last of the statements in the main drawing room. Judge Planche asked:

'Have you gone up to see her?'

It was obvious he meant Madame Fumal.

'Not yet.'

He needed to do that. He also needed to question Félix and the rest of the staff. And find Roger Gaillardin and question this Martine Gilloux, who might have a key to the small door.

And finally he needed to go to the offices on Rue Rambuteau and at La Villette and gather all the testimony that might be relevant . . .

Maigret was already disheartened. He felt he had got off to a bad start. Fumal had asked for his protection. He hadn't believed him, and Fumal had been shot in the back.

Any moment now the minister of the interior would be ringing the commissioner of the Police Judiciaire.

As if the Englishwoman vanishing into thin air wasn't enough!

Louise Bourges was looking at him from across the room as if she was trying to guess what he was thinking. He was thinking about her, as it happened, wondering if she had really seen her employer writing one of the anonymous notes.

If she hadn't, that changed everything.

4. The Drunk Woman and the Photographer with the Muffled Tread

Almost thirty years earlier, when Maigret, newly married, was still the secretary of the police station in Rue de Rochechouart, his wife would sometimes come and meet him at the office at midday. They would make do with a quick bite for lunch so they'd have time for a walk along the backstreets and boulevards, and Maigret remembered coming in spring to this same Parc Monceau that he could now see, in black and white, outside Fumal's windows.

There had been more nannies back then, the majority in smart uniforms. The babies' prams exuded an air of luxurious comfort, the iron chairs on the paths were freshly painted yellow, and an old lady with a hat trimmed with violets was feeding bread to the birds.

'When I'm detective chief inspector . . .' he had joked.

And both of them had looked through the railings, with their gilded spikes glinting in the sun, at the opulent townhouses around the park, imagining the elegant, harmonious lives people must be living behind their windows.

If there was anyone in Paris who had gained first-hand experience of life's brutal realities, who had learned, day after day, how to discover the truth of appearances, it was him, and yet he had never entirely grown out of certain fantasies from his childhood and adolescence.

Hadn't he once said that he would have liked to be a 'mender of destinies', such was his desire to restore people to their rightful places, the places they would have occupied if the world were a naive, picture postcard version of itself?

Conflict rather than harmony probably reigned in eight out of ten of the still magnificent houses that surrounded the park. But he had rarely had the opportunity to breathe such a strained atmosphere as the one between these walls. Everything seemed fake, grating, starting with the lodge of the concierge-cum-manservant, who was neither a concierge nor a manservant, despite his striped waistcoat, but a former poacher, a murderer turned guard dog.

What about that shady bailiff Monsieur Joseph, what was he doing up in the attic?

Louise Bourges didn't inspire confidence either, with her dreams of marrying the chauffeur and opening an inn in Gien.

But Saint-Fiacre's erstwhile butcher was the most out of place of them all, and his every attempt at decoration – the high panelled walls, the furniture that he'd probably bought at the same time as the house – seemed as incongruous as the two statues flanking the landing.

What may have troubled Maigret the most was the malice he sensed in everything Fumal did, because he had always refused to believe in pure evil.

It was after ten o'clock when he left the first floor where his colleagues were still working and started slowly up the stairs. On the second floor, there was no sign of a maid to prevent him pushing open the door of a drawing room that boasted fifteen or sixteen empty armchairs. He coughed to signal his presence.

No one came. Nothing stirred. He headed towards a half-open door which gave on to a smaller sitting room in which a breakfast tray lay on a pedestal table.

He knocked at a third door. Straining to hear, he thought he heard a stifled cough and ended up turning the door knob.

It was Madame Fumal's bedroom. She was lying in bed and, as he walked towards her, she watched him with a dazed look.

'I'm sorry. I didn't see anyone who could let you know I was here. I imagine all the maids are downstairs with my inspectors.'

She hadn't combed her hair or washed. Her nightdress left most of her shoulders and part of a pallid breast bare. He might have had his doubts the day before, but now he was certain that he was looking at a woman who had been drinking not only before she went to sleep but also since she had woken up that morning. A strong reek of alcohol still hung in the air.

The butcher's wife carried on looking at him in an ambiguous way, as if, although not yet entirely reassured, she was feeling a certain relief, even a secret merriment.

'I imagine you've been told?'

She nodded, and her eyes flashed with something other than grief.

'Your husband is dead. Someone killed him.'

In a slightly hoarse voice, she declared:

'I always thought it would end like this.'

She giggled a little, clearly even drunker than he'd thought when he came in.

'Did you expect him to be murdered?'

'I was prepared for anything with him.'

Gesturing towards the messy bed, the untidy bedroom, she stammered:

'I'm sorry . . .'

'Haven't you been curious enough to go downstairs?'

'Why?'

The look in her eye suddenly became sharper.

'He's really dead, isn't he?'

When he nodded, she slipped her hand under the blankets, took out a bottle and brought it to her lips.

'To his health!' she joked.

But Fumal still scared her even when he was dead. She looked fearfully at the door and asked Maigret:

'Is he still in the house?'

'They've just taken him to the Forensic Institute.'

'What are they going to do to him?'

'The autopsy.'

Was it the news that her husband's body was going to be cut open that made her break into an impish smile? Did that represent a sort of vengeance for her, compensation for everything she had suffered at his hands?

She must have been a perfectly ordinary girl and young woman. What had Fumal put her through to reduce her to such a pitiful state?

Maigret had come across wrecks like her before but usually in sordid settings, deprived neighbourhoods, where poverty was invariably at the root of their degradation.

'Did he come and see you yesterday evening?'

'Who?'

'Your husband.'

She shook her head.

'Did he sometimes?'

'Sometimes, yes, but I'd rather have never had to see him.'

'Didn't you ever go down to his office?'

'Never. That was where he saw my father for the last time, and three hours later my father was found hanged.'

That was Fumal's vice, apparently: ruining people, not only those who were in his way or causing him trouble but anyone he could, to assert his power, convince himself of it.

'Do you know who paid him a visit last night?'

Maigret would have to get an inspector to search her apartment in due course. The thought of doing it himself repelled him, but it had to be done. There was nothing to prove that this woman hadn't finally got up the courage to kill her husband. It wasn't out of the question that the murder weapon would be found in her rooms.

'I don't know . . . I don't want to know any more . . . Do you know what I want? To be left alone and . . .'

Maigret didn't hear what she was saying. Still standing near her bed, he saw Madame Fumal's gaze fix on a point behind him. There was a glare as a flashbulb went off, and at the same moment she threw back the covers and, with an energy he hadn't imagined she possessed, hurled herself at a photographer who had silently appeared in the doorway.

The man tried to back away, but she had already grabbed

the camera and thrown it furiously to the floor. Then she picked it up and smashed it on the ground again even more violently.

Maigret had recognized the reporter from one of the evening papers. He frowned. Someone, he didn't know who, had tipped off the press. They would be out in force when he went downstairs.

'One moment . . .' he said firmly.

He picked up the camera himself and took out the film.

'Out you go, son . . .' he said to the young man.

And to Madame Fumal:

'Go back to bed. I'm sorry for what's happened. I'll see that you're left in peace from now on. One of my men will have to inspect your apartment, though.'

He couldn't wait to get out of that room – and the whole house, if it was up to him – and never come back. The photographer was waiting for him on the landing.

'I thought I could . . .'

'You pushed it a bit too far. Are your colleagues here?'

'A few.'

'Who told them?'

'I don't know. About half an hour ago my editor in chief sent for me . . .'

The clerk at the Forensic Institute probably. There were people hand in glove with the newspapers like that almost everywhere.

Seven or eight representatives of the press were already in attendance downstairs, and others were on their way.

'What happened exactly, detective chief inspector?'

'If I knew, I wouldn't be here. I'm going to ask you to

let us work in peace and I promise you that if we find anything . . .'

'Can we take photographs?'

'Be quick.'

There were too many people to question to take them to Quai des Orfèvres, so a big, empty suite of rooms had been pressed into service instead. Lapointe was already at work with Bonfils, and Torrence had just arrived with Lesueur.

He assigned the job of searching the apartment on the second floor to Torrence and sent Bonfils up to Monsieur Joseph's rooms. Fumal's business manager hadn't returned from Rue Rambuteau yet.

'When he gets back, question him, just in case, but I doubt he'll say much.'

The gentlemen from the public prosecutor's office had left, as had most of the specialists from Criminal Records.

'Send a maid up to see to Madame Fumal – just one, Noémi, she always does it – and have the others wait in the drawing room.'

When the telephone rang in the dead man's office, it was Louise Bourges, unsurprisingly, who answered.

'Monsieur Fumal's secretary here . . . Yes . . . Of course, he's here . . . I'll put him on . . .'

She turned towards Maigret.

'It's for you . . . From Quai des Orfèvres . . .'

'Hello, yes . . .'

The commissioner of the Police Judiciaire was on the other end of the line.

'The minister of the interior has just rung . . .'

'Does he know?'

'Yes. Everyone does.'

Had one of the journalists told radio news? It was possible.

'Is he furious?'

'That's not the word. Bothered, more like it. He wants to be kept regularly updated about the investigation as it progresses. Have you got any ideas?'

'None.'

'People think it'll cause an uproar. That man was an even bigger wheel than he claimed to be.'

'Will he be missed?'

'Why do you ask that?'

'No reason. So far people seem relieved, if anything.'

'You're pulling out all the stops, aren't you?'

Of course he was! And yet he'd never felt so little desire to find the murderer. Admittedly he was curious to know who had finally decided to do away with Fumal, who had reached the end of his or her tether and staked everything. But would he hold it against them? Wasn't it more likely he'd feel a pang of anguish when he put the handcuffs on?

He had rarely been faced with so many hypotheses, each as plausible as the next.

There was Madame Fumal, obviously, who would have only had to go down one floor to avenge herself for twenty years of humiliation. Besides regaining her freedom, she would probably stand to inherit his fortune, either outright or in part.

Did she have a lover? Judging by appearances it seemed unlikely, but it was a subject on which he had become increasingly sceptical.

Then there was Monsieur Joseph . . .

He seemed utterly devoted to the wholesale butcher, in whose shadow he lived. Lord knows what schemes they'd got up to, those two. Fumal must have had some sort of a hold over the fellow, mustn't he, as he seemed to over everyone who worked for him?

But even creatures like Monsieur Joseph rebel!

What about Louise Bourges, the secretary who had come to see him at Quai des Orfèvres?

So far she was the only person to claim that her employer had written the anonymous notes himself.

Félix, the chauffeur, was her lover. Both were in a hurry to get married and move to Giens.

Supposing she or Félix had robbed Fumal, or tried to swindle, even blackmail him?

Everybody in this business seemed to have reasons to commit murder, including Victor, the former poacher, who was kept on a tight leash by his boss.

They would pore over the lives of all the other staff. Not to mention Gaillardin, who hadn't returned to Rue François Premier after visiting Fumal.

'Are you leaving, chief?'

'I'll be back in a few minutes.'

He was thirsty and needed to fill his lungs with something other than the air in that house.

'If anyone asks for me, tell Lapointe to take a message.'

On the landing, he had to fend off the journalists and downstairs he found several press cars and a radio car by the side of the road. A handful of passers-by had stopped, and a uniformed policeman was standing in front of the door.

With his hands in his pockets, Maigret walked fast towards Boulevard des Batignolles, where he went into the first bistro he came across.

'A beer,' he ordered. 'And a token.'

The token was to telephone his wife.

'I definitely won't be back for lunch . . . Dinner? I hope so . . . Maybe . . . No, I'm not annoyed about anything . . .'

Maybe the minister was actually pretty happy to be rid of a compromising friend, he thought. And other people must have been thrilled. The staff at Rue Rambuteau, say, and La Villette, and all the managers of the butchers' shops whose lives Fumal had made hell.

He didn't yet know that the newspapers' afternoon editions would proclaim:

King of Meat Trade Murdered

Newspapers are fond of the word 'king', as they are of 'millionaire'. One paper would specify that, according to experts, Fumal controlled a tenth of the butchery trade in Paris and more than a quarter in certain départements in the north.

Who was going to inherit that empire? Madame Fumal?

As he was coming out of the bistro Maigret saw a taxi with its light on, which gave him the idea of going and having a look around Rue François Premier. He had already sent Neveu there, whom he hadn't heard from, but he wanted to see for himself and, above all, he was glad to have an excuse to escape the nauseating atmosphere of Boulevard de Courcelles for a while.

It was a modern block, with a smart, almost luxurious concierge's lodge.

'Monsieur Gaillardin? Third floor on the left, but I don't think he's at home.'

Maigret took the lift, rang the bell. A young woman in a dressing gown came to open the door, or rather hold it open a crack until he said his name.

'Still no word from Roger?' she asked, showing him into a living room as full of light as any room in Paris could be in that weather.

'Have you heard anything?'

'No. I've been worried since your inspector came here. Just now I heard on the radio . . .'

'Did they mention Fumal?'

'Yes.'

'Did you know your husband went to see him yesterday evening?'

She was pretty, with a delectable figure, and can't have been much over thirty.

'He's not my husband,' she corrected him. 'Roger and I aren't married.'

'I know. I didn't mean to say that.'

'He has a wife and two children but he doesn't live with them. He hasn't for years . . . wait . . . for five years exactly.'

'Are you aware of his problems?'

'I know he's more or less ruined and that that man . . .'

'Tell me, does Gaillardin have a revolver?'

She paled visibly, making it impossible for her to lie.

'There's always been one in his drawer.'

'Will you check if it's still there? May I come with you?'

He followed her into the bedroom, where she had evidently slept alone in a huge, very low bed. She opened two or three drawers and seemed surprised, then started opening other drawers increasingly feverishly.

'I can't find it.'

'I don't suppose he ever carried it on him?'

'Not that I know of. You don't know him, do you? He's a calm person, very cheerful, what people would call a bon vivant.'

'Weren't you worried when you saw he hadn't come home?'

She didn't know what to say.

'Yes . . . Of course . . . I told your inspector I was . . . But, you see, he was confident . . . He was sure he'd find the money in the nick of time . . . I thought he'd gone to see some friends, maybe out of town.'

'Where does his wife live?'

'In Neuilly. I'll give you her address.'

She wrote it down on a piece of paper for him. The telephone rang just then. Apologizing, she picked it up. The voice on the other end of the line was so booming that Maigret could hear what it was saying.

'Hello? Madame Gaillardin?'

'Yes . . . I mean . . .'

'Is this 26, Rue François Premier?'

'Yes.'

'The residence of a Roger Gaillardin?'

Maigret would have sworn the invisible speaker was a duty sergeant in a police station.

'Yes. I live with him but I'm not his wife.'

'Could you come to Puteaux station as soon as possible?'

'Has something happened?'

'Something's happened, yes.'

'Is Roger dead?'

'Yes.'

'Can't you tell me what happened?'

'First you've got to identify the body. We've found some identity papers, but . . .'

Maigret signalled to the young woman to hand him the receiver.

'Hello, this is Detective Chief Inspector Maigret, Police Judiciaire. Tell me what you know.'

'At nine thirty-two a man was found dead on the banks of the Seine, 300 metres downstream from the Pont de Puteaux. A pile of bricks unloaded a few days ago prevented passers-by from noticing him earlier. It was a bargee who . . .'

'Murdered?'

'No. At least, I don't think so, because he was still holding a revolver with only one bullet missing. He appears to have shot himself in the right temple.'

'Thank you. When the body has been identified, send it to the Forensic Institute and get the contents of his pockets sent over to Quai des Orfèvres. The person who answered just now will meet you there.'

Maigret hung up.

'He shot himself in the head,' he said.

'I heard.'

'Does his wife have a telephone?'

'Yes.'

She gave him the number, which he dialled.

'Hello, Madame Gaillardin?'

'It's the maid here.'

'Isn't Madame Gaillardin at home?'

'She left for the Côte d'Azur the day before yesterday with her children. Who's speaking? Is that monsieur?'

'No. The police. I have a question. Were you in the apartment yesterday evening?'

'Of course.'

'Did Monsieur Gaillardin come by?'

'Why?'

'Please answer.'

'The answer is yes.'

'What time?'

'I was in bed. It was after ten thirty.'

'What did he want?'

'To talk to madame.'

'Did he often visit in the evening?'

'Not in the evening, no.'

'In the day?'

'He'd come and see the children.'

'But yesterday he wanted to talk to his wife?'

'Yes. He seemed surprised that she'd gone away.'

'Did he stay long?'

'No.'

'Did he seem agitated?'

'Definitely tired. I even offered him a glass of cognac.'

'Did he drink it?'

'In one.'

Maigret hung up, turned towards the young woman.

'You can go to Puteaux.'

'Aren't you coming with me?'

'Not now. I'm sure I'll have the chance to see you again.'

So, to sum up, Gaillardin had left Rue François Premier the previous day, taking his revolver with him, and headed to Boulevard de Courcelles first. Did he hope Fumal would give him a stay of execution? Was he counting on some argument to sway him?

He can't have had any luck. Shortly afterwards he had rung the bell of his wife's apartment in Neuilly and only found the maid at home. The apartment was near the Seine. Three hundred metres away was the Pont de Puteaux. He had walked across the bridge.

Had he roamed around on the embankments for a long time before shooting himself in the head?

Maigret went into a upmarket-looking bar and muttered, 'A beer and a token.'

The token was to call the Forensic Institute.

'Maigret here. Has Doctor Paul arrived? What? Maigret, yes . . . He's still busy? Ask him if he's found the bullet . . . Wait . . . If he's found it, see if it's from a revolver or an automatic . . .'

He heard people moving around, voices on the other end of the line.

'Hello . . . Detective chief inspector? The bullet appears to be from an automatic . . . It lodged in . . .'

75

He wasn't interested where the bullet that killed Fumal had lodged.

Short of assuming Roger Gaillardin had been carrying two guns that evening, he can't have been the person who killed the king of the meat trade.

As he crossed the landing on the first floor at Boulevard de Courcelles, he was set upon by the journalists again. To get rid of them, he told them about the discovery on the embankment at Puteaux.

The inspectors were still questioning the secretary and staff in different rooms. Torrence was the only one at a loose end. He seemed to be waiting impatiently for Maigret and immediately drew him into a corner.

'I've found something upstairs, chief,' he said in a low voice.

'The firearm?'

'No. Come with me, will you?'

They went up to the second floor, entered the drawing room with all the armchairs and the piano that must have been purely ornamental.

'In Madame Fumal's bedroom?'

Torrence shook his head mysteriously.

'Her apartment is huge,' he muttered. 'You'll see.'

With the assurance of someone who knows his way around, he pointed out the different rooms to Maigret, without worrying about Madame Fumal, who was still in bed.

'I haven't told her anything yet. I think it's better if it comes from you. This way . . .'

They went through one empty bedroom, then another, both of which clearly hadn't been slept in for a long time. There was a disused bathroom as well, which had been used to store buckets and brooms.

Down a corridor, on the left, a sizeable room was stacked full of furniture, trunks and dusty suitcases.

Finally, at the very end of the corridor, Torrence opened the door to a room that was smaller and narrower than the others, with a single window giving on to the courtyard. It was furnished like a maid's room, with a couch covered in red rep, a table, two chairs and a cheap wardrobe. The inspector, a triumphant glint in his eyes, pointed to a promotional ashtray in which two cigarette butts could be seen.

'Smell them, chief. I don't know what Moers will say but I'd swear those cigarettes weren't smoked long ago. Yesterday probably. Maybe even this morning. When I came in the room still smelled of tobacco.'

'Have you had a look in the wardrobe?'

'There's only a couple of blankets. Now, get up on the chair . . . Watch out, it's wobbly.'

Maigret knew from experience that most people who want to hide an object put it on top of a wardrobe or cupboard. And on top of this one, on a thick layer of dust, were a razor, a packet of razor blades and a tube of shaving foam.

'What do you say to that?'

'You haven't talked to the staff about this, have you?'

'I preferred to wait for you.'

'Go back to the drawing room.'

Maigret knocked on the door of the bedroom. There was no answer but when he pushed it open, he found Madame Fumal's eyes trained on him.

'What do you want now? Can't I be left to sleep?'

She was no better or worse than she had been that morning. If she had been drinking again, it hardly showed.

'I'm sorry to disturb you, but I have to do my job and I've got a few questions to ask you.'

She was still frowning at him, as if she was trying to guess what was coming next.

'I believe all the servants sleep in the rooms above the garage, isn't that so?'

'Yes. Why?'

'Do you smoke?'

She hesitated but hadn't time to think of a lie.

'No.'

'Do you always sleep in this room?'

'What do you mean?'

'I imagine your husband never came to sleep in your part of the house either?'

This time it was obvious that she had understood and, abandoning her defensive attitude, she shrank down even further under the sheets.

'Is he still there?' she asked in a low voice.

'No. I have reason to believe that he spent at least part of the night there.'

'Maybe. I don't know when he left. He comes and goes . . .'

'Who is it?'

She seemed surprised. She must have thought he was better informed and now seemed to regret saying too much.

'Hasn't anyone told you?'

'Who could have?'

'Noémi . . . Or Germaine . . . They both know . . . Although Noémi . . .'

A strange smile hovered on her lips.

'Is it your lover?'

She burst out laughing – a shout of harsh, racking laughter.

'Can you see me with a lover? You think a man would still want me, do you? Have you looked at me, inspector? Do you want to see what . . .'

Her hand tensed on the sheet as if she was going to pull it back, and Maigret was afraid for a moment that she was going to show him her naked body.

'My lover!' she repeated. 'No, inspector. I don't have a lover. It's been a long time since . . .'

She realized she was revealing too much.

'I've had some, it's true. And Ferdinand knew. And he made me pay for it my whole life. You had to pay for everything with him, everything. Do you understand? But my brother has never done anything to him apart from being my father's son and my brother.'

'Your brother slept in the room at the back, did he?'

'Yes. He often sleeps there. A few times a week, maybe. Whenever he makes it this far.'

'What does he do?'

She looked him hard in the eye with a sort of suppressed fury.

'He drinks!' she cried. 'Like me! There's nothing else left for him to do. He had money, a wife, children . . .'

'Did your husband ruin him?'

'He took his last centime. But if you're thinking it was my brother who killed him, you're wrong. He's not physically up to anything like that any more. Nor am I.'

'Where is he now?'

She shrugged.

'Somewhere where there's a bar. He's not young any more. He's fifty-two and looks at least sixty-five. His children, who are married, refuse to see him. His wife works in Limoges.'

Her hand groped for the bottle.

'Did Victor let him into the house?'

'If Victor had known, he would have gone and told my husband.'

'Did your brother have a key?'

'Noémi had one made for him.'

'What is your brother's name?'

'Émile . . . Émile Lentin . . . I can't tell you where you'll find him. When he finds out from the papers that Fumal is dead, he probably won't dare come here. In that case you'll end up picking him up by the river or at the Salvation Army.'

She gave him another defiant look and, with a bitter set to her mouth, started drinking from the bottle.

5. The Woman Who Likes the Fireside and the Girl Who Likes a Good Meal

He didn't need to say who he was or show his badge. A glass peephole at head height in the middle of the door allowed the person inside to see who was ringing. The door opened immediately, and a voice cried in raptures:

'Monsieur Maigret!'

The recognition was mutual as the woman opened the door for him and showed him into a sweltering room with a gas radiator on full blast. She must have been at least sixty but she had hardly changed since the time Maigret had rescued her from a tricky situation when she was running a discreet brothel in Rue Notre-Dame-de-Lorette.

He didn't expect to find her presiding over this short-stay hotel on Rue de l'Étoile, with its sign saying, 'Luxury studios by the month and week'.

Not that it was a hotel, strictly speaking. The office wasn't much of an office either, more of a boudoir with comfy armchairs and silk cushions on which two or three Persian cats sat purring. Rose's hair was sparser, although still peroxide blonde, her face and body plumper, her skin slightly waxy.

'Who are you here for?' she asked, rushing excitedly to clear one of the chairs. She'd always had a soft spot for

Maigret, whom she'd go and see at Quai des Orfèvres in the old days whenever she had a problem.

'Do you have a Martine Gilloux here?'

It was midday. The newspapers hadn't reported Fumal's death yet. In what he thought was a slightly cowardly way, Maigret had again left his colleagues working in the depressing atmosphere of Boulevard de Courcelles and made his second getaway of the morning.

'I don't suppose she's done anything wrong, has she?' she said, adding hurriedly, 'She's a good girl, completely harmless.'

'Is she upstairs at the moment?'

'She went out maybe quarter of an hour ago. She doesn't like going to bed late, that one. At this time of the morning she goes and takes a little turn round the neighbourhood before having lunch at Gino's or some other restaurant on Place des Ternes.'

The little sitting room looked like the one at Rue Notre-Dame-de-Lorette, minus the erotic engravings on the walls that had been part of the tools of the trade there, and it was just as hot. Rose had always felt the cold, or rather had always liked heat for heat's sake, overheating her rooms and swathing herself in quilted dressing gowns. Sometimes she'd go weeks in winter without poking her nose outdoors.

'Has she lived here for a long time?'

'Over a year.'

'What sort of girl is she?'

They spoke the same language and understood one another.

'A good kid who hasn't had any luck for years. She's from a very poor family. She was born somewhere in the suburbs, I can't remember where, but she told me she went hungry a lot, and I could tell she wasn't making it up.'

She asked again:

'Is it something bad?'

'I don't think so.'

'I'm sure it isn't. She's not really very bright and tries to be nice to everybody. Men take advantage of her. She's had her ups and downs, especially downs. For a long time, she was at the beck and call of a thug who put her through hell and luckily for her ended up getting sent down. She told me all this herself, because she wasn't living here at the time but somewhere over by Barbès. She happened to find someone who got her a studio here with me and since then she's been fine.'

'Fumal?'

'That's his name, yes. A big-shot butcher, who has several cars and a chauffeur.'

'Does he visit regularly?'

'He sometimes goes two or three days without coming, then we see him every afternoon or evening.'

'Anything else?'

'I can't think of anything. You know the deal. He gives her a nice allowance without going crazy. She has a few pretty dresses, a fur coat, two or three pieces of jewellery.'

'Does he go out with her?'

'Sometimes, especially when he's having dinner in town with friends who have partners.'

'Does Martine have another boyfriend?'

'I wondered that myself at the start. It's rare that those girls don't feel the need to have someone. I asked her some sly questions – I always find out what's happening round here in the end – and believe you me, she hasn't got anybody. She finds it more relaxing that way. At heart, she's not very keen on men.'

'No drugs?'

'That's not her style.'

'How does she spend her time?'

'She stays in, reading or listening to the radio. She sleeps. She goes out to eat, goes for a little walk and comes back.'

'Do you know Fumal?'

'I've seen him go past in the corridor. The car and the chauffeur often wait outside while he's up there.'

'Did you say that I'll find her at Gino's?'

'Do you know it? A little Italian restaurant . . .'

Maigret knew it. The restaurant wasn't large or showy but it was famous for its pasta, especially its ravioli, and had a select clientele.

When he got there, he stopped at the bar first.

'Is Martine Gilloux here?'

There were already a dozen male and female customers. The barman winked in the direction of a young woman who was having lunch alone in a corner.

Leaving his overcoat and hat at the cloakroom, Maigret went over to her, rested his hand on the unoccupied chair on the other side of the table and asked:

'May I?'

She looked at him uncomprehendingly, so he said:

'I need to talk to you. I'm from the police.'

There were a dozen small hors-d'oeuvres dishes in front of her, he noticed.

'Don't be afraid. It's just a few questions.'

'About who?'

'About Fumal. And you.'

He turned towards the head waiter, who had come over.

'Give me some hors-d'oeuvres too, then a spaghetti Milanese.'

Finally he told the young woman, who was looking stunned as well as anxious now:

'I've come from Rue de l'Étoile. Rose told me that I would find you here. Fumal is dead.'

She must have been between twenty-five and twenty-eight, but there was something older in the look in her eyes: tiredness and indifference, maybe a lack of curiosity about life. She was fairly tall, rather large, with a gentle, timid expression which reminded you of a child who's been beaten.

'Didn't you know?'

She shook her head, still looking at him without knowing what to think.

'Did you see him yesterday?'

'Wait . . . Yesterday . . . Yes . . . He came to see me around five . . .'

'How was he?'

'The same as usual.'

Something had just struck Maigret. Until now, although

85

they kept it pretty well hidden, everyone he talked to had been amazed and delighted when they heard about Fumal's death. At the very least, you sensed they were relieved.

But Martine Gilloux received the news gravely, possibly with a hint of sadness, definitely anxiously.

Was she thinking that her fate hung in the balance again, that her peace and comfort were over, perhaps for good? Was she afraid of going back to the streets, where she had spent so much of her life?

'Go on eating,' he said to her, as his order was brought.

She did so mechanically and he realized that eating was the most important thing in life for her, her principal source of reassurance. She had probably been eating intently for the last year to erase the memory of all the years she had gone hungry, or avenge it.

'What do you know about him?' he asked quietly.

'Are you sure you're from the police?'

She was on the verge of asking the barman or head waiter, who were watching them, for advice. He held out his badge.

'Detective Chief Inspector Maigret,' he said.

'I've seen your name in the papers before. Is that you? I thought you'd be fatter.'

'Tell me about Fumal. Start at the beginning. Where did you meet him, when, how?'

'Just over a year ago.'

'Where?'

'In a little club in Montmartre, Le Désir. I was at the bar. He came in with some friends who had drunk more than him.'

'Didn't he drink?'

'I never saw him drunk.'

'Then what?'

'There were other girls there. One of his friends called one over. Then another guy, a butcher, I think, from Lille or somewhere in the north, came and got my friend Nina. He was the only one left at their table on his own. So, he waved to me across the room to come over. You know how it goes. I could see he wasn't really that keen, that he just wanted to be like the others. I remember that he looked at me and said, "You're thin. You must be hungry."

'It's true, I was thin at that point. Without asking me, he called the maitre d' and ordered me a full dinner.

' "Eat! Drink! It's not every night you'll get the chance to meet Fumal."

'That's pretty much how it started. His friends left before him with the two other girls. He asked me questions about my parents, my childhood, what I was doing. You often get ones like that. He didn't even feel me up.'

'In the end, he decided:

' "Come on! I'm going to take you to a decent hotel." '

'Did he spend the night there?' asked Maigret.

'No. It was near Place Clichy, I remember. He paid a week in advance, and that night he didn't even come up to the room. He came back the next day.'

'Did he come up that time?'

'Yes. He stayed for a while. But not so much for what you think. He wasn't very good at that. He mainly talked to me about himself, what he was doing, his wife.'

'What did he say about her?'

'I think he was unhappy.'

Maigret could hardly believe his ears.

'Go on,' he muttered, automatically assuming a more familiar tone.

'It's hard, you understand? He talked to me about all that so often . . .'

'So, he really came to see you to talk about her.'

'Not only that . . .'

'But mainly?'

'Maybe. Apparently, he'd worked a lot, more than anyone in the whole world, and he'd become a very powerful man. Is that true?'

'It *was* true, yes.'

'He'd say things to me like:

' "What good is it to me? People have no idea who I am and think I'm a lout. My wife's crazy. All my staff and employees think about is how to steal from me. And when I go into a fashionable restaurant I can tell people are muttering: 'Look, there's the butcher!' " '

The waiter brought spaghetti for Maigret and ravioli for Martine Gilloux, who had a flask of Chianti on the table in front of her.

'Do you mind?'

Her worries did not prevent her eating heartily.

'He said that his wife was crazy?'

'And that she loathed him. He bought the chateau in the village where he was born. Is that true too?'

'It is.'

'You know, I didn't take any of it that seriously. I thought that some of it was probably boasting. The locals still call him The Butcher. He bought a townhouse on Boulevard de Courcelles and he used to say that it felt like a railway station rather than a home.'

'Did you go there?'

'Yes.'

'Do you have a key?'

'No. I only went there twice. The first time because he wanted to show me where he lived. It was one night. We went up to the first floor. I saw the big drawing room, his office, his bedroom, the dining room, then some other rooms, which were almost empty. It's true, it didn't feel like a real home.

' "The madwoman's up there," he said. "She'll be on the landing spying on us."

'I asked him if she was jealous and he said that she wasn't, that she spied on him just for the hell of it, that it was her obsession. Is it true that she drinks?'

'Yes.'

'In that case, you see, almost everything he told me is true. Does that include him being able to walk into ministers' offices unannounced?'

'That's hardly an exaggeration.'

Wasn't there something ironic about Fumal and Martine's relationship? For over a year, she had been his mistress. He'd hardly slept with her, really, and only kept her on as an audience before whom he could show off and complain.

Some men, when they have too much weighing on their hearts, pick up a prostitute in the street just so they can confide in her.

Fumal went one further, buying an exclusive personal confidante and setting her up in style in Rue de l'Étoile so that her only job was to wait on his pleasure.

At heart, though, she had never really believed him. Not only that but she'd never even wondered if what he told her was true or false.

She didn't care!

Now that he was dead she was overawed to learn that he had genuinely been the heavyweight he wanted people to think he was.

'He wasn't worried lately, was he?'

'What do you mean?'

'Was he afraid for his life? Did he talk about his enemies?'

'He often told me that you can't become powerful without making a lot of enemies. He used to say:

' "They can lick my hands like dogs all they want but deep down they all loathe me, and the day I die will be the happiest day of their lives."

'Then he'd add:

' "It will be yours too, come to that. Or it would be if I left you something. But I'm not going to leave you anything. Maybe I'll die or maybe I'll drop you, but either way you'll go back to the gutter." '

She wasn't shocked. She had been through too much before she met him. He had bought her a few months of security, and that was enough for her.

'What happened to him?' it was her turn to ask. 'Was it his heart?'

'Did he have a bad heart?'

'I don't know. When people die suddenly, they usually say . . .'

'He was murdered.'

She stopped eating, so stunned that her mouth hung open. It was a while before she could ask:

'Where? When?'

'Yesterday evening. At his house.'

'Who did it?'

'That's what I'm trying to find out.'

'How did they do it?'

'A revolver bullet.'

She had lost her appetite, probably for the first time in her life. She pushed her plate away and reached for her glass, draining it in one.

'Just my luck,' he heard her mutter.

'Did he ever talk about a Monsieur Joseph?'

'A little old man?'

'Yes.'

'He called him The Thief. Apparently, he really was one. Ferdinand could have had him put in jail, but he preferred to keep him on his payroll, saying that crooks do a better job than upright citizens. He even moved him into the attic so he always had him to hand.'

'And his secretary?'

'Mademoiselle Louise?'

So Fumal really had confided in his mistress in detail.

'What did he think of her?'

'That she was cold, ambitious, greedy, and that she was only working for him for the money.'

'Anything else?'

'Yes. Something happened with her. Has she told you?'

'Go on.'

'What's the harm! He's dead now . . .'

She looked around and lowered her voice so the head waiter wouldn't hear.

'One day at the office he pretended to be making a pass at her, started groping her, then ordered:

' "Take your clothes off." '

'Did she obey?' Maigret asked, surprised.

'He said she did. He didn't even take her to his bedroom. He stayed standing by the window as she stripped, watching her with an ironic expression. When she was naked, he asked her:

' "Are you a virgin?" '

'What did she say?'

'Nothing. She blushed. After a while he muttered:

' "You're not a virgin. That'll do. Put your clothes back on." '

'I didn't believe that story at the time. People have abused me too. But I never had any teaching or education. Men know they can take any liberty they like with me. But a girl like her . . .

'If he wasn't lying, he watched her get dressed again, pointed her to her chair and shorthand pad, then started dictating a letter to her . . .'

'Do you have a lover?' Maigret asked point-blank.

She denied it strongly, but, as she did so, she looked in the barman's direction.

'Is that him?'

'No.'

'Are you in love with him?'

'It's not love.'

'But it wouldn't take much, would it?'

'I don't know. He won't have anything to do with me.'

He ordered coffee, asked Martine:

'No dessert?'

'Not today. I feel so queasy I'm going to go to bed. Do you need me any more?'

'No. Leave it. I'll take care of the bill. Until you hear differently you're not to leave Rue de l'Étoile.'

'Even for meals?'

'Only for meals.'

The inspectors had had lunch at a little Norman restaurant they had found near Boulevard de Courcelles and were already back at work when Maigret arrived.

There were several pieces of unimportant news. It had been confirmed that Roger Gaillardin had committed suicide and that the revolver hadn't been slipped into his hand after he died. It was the same gun he used to keep in the apartment on Rue François Premier.

The firearms expert also stated that the automatic found in Fumal's bedroom hadn't been used for months, probably years.

Lucas and Monsieur Joseph had returned from Rue Rambuteau, where confusion reigned.

'There's nobody to give instructions and no one knows what's going to happen. Fumal hated delegating power. He ran everything himself, would suddenly show up when he was least expected, and his employees lived in a constant state of dread. The only person, apparently, who knows what's what is Monsieur Joseph, but he has no legal authority and is as loathed as his boss was.'

The latest editions of the papers that had just come out confirmed this state of affairs.

Almost all had the same headline:

King of Meat Trade Murdered
A man with a very low public profile who nonetheless played a considerable role . . .

They listed the companies he had set up, which, with their branches and subsidiaries, constituted a veritable empire.

They recalled, which Maigret didn't know, that five years earlier this empire had almost collapsed when the tax authorities had done some digging into Fumal's affairs. A scandal had been avoided, although the word in informed circles was of tax fraud amounting to over a billion francs.

How had it been hushed up? The newspapers didn't say, but the implication was that the former butcher of Saint-Fiacre had friends in high places.

One of the papers asked:

Will his death reopen the case?

At all events, some people must have been feeling uneasy that afternoon, including the minister who had telephoned the Police Judiciaire.

What the newspapers still did not know, but perhaps

would find out, was that the previous day the aforementioned Fumal had asked the police to protect him.

Had Maigret done everything in his power to keep him safe?

He had sent an inspector to guard the house on Boulevard de Courcelles, which was standard procedure in such cases. He had gone to the trouble of casting an eye over the premises and put Lapointe in charge of shadowing Fumal wherever he went, starting the following morning. They had been about to continue the investigation when . . .

He hadn't made any professional mistakes. But that didn't make him any less dissatisfied with himself. Hadn't he, for a start, let his judgement be influenced by memories of his childhood, in particular by the way Fumal's father had behaved towards his own father?

He hadn't afforded the man who had come to see him on the minister of the interior's recommendation any sympathy.

But when Louise Bourges, his secretary, had appeared, he hadn't doubted her word for a minute.

Similarly, he was convinced that the story Martine had just told him in the restaurant was true. Ferdinand Fumal was exactly the sort of man who would humiliate a woman in a sickening way. It was nonetheless true, however, that the secretary felt nothing but contempt – or hatred – for him, and that she was working for him purely so that she could marry Félix and that they could save enough money to buy an inn in Gien.

Did she make do with her wages? Didn't her proximity

to Fumal, and the fact she was privy to his business secrets, mean she had other ways to make money?

The man used to say to his mistress:

'All anyone thinks about is how to steal from me . . .'

Was he so far off the mark? Maigret hadn't yet met anyone who showed the slightest affection for him. They were all working for him under protest.

Nor did Fumal do anything to make himself lovable. Quite the opposite. It was as if he took a malign pleasure, a secret delight in provoking hatred. And he clearly hadn't been feeling hatred coming at him from all sides just for a few days, or a few weeks, or even a few years.

So why was it only yesterday that he had felt so worried that he had asked for police protection?

Why, if his secretary wasn't lying, had he gone to the trouble of sending himself anonymous threats?

Had he suddenly discovered that he had a more dangerous enemy than the ones he already knew about? Or had he given someone especially urgent reasons to kill him?

It was possible. Moers was studying specimens of Fumal's and Louise Bourges' handwriting along with the threats. He had called in one of the best experts in Paris to assist him.

Sluggish and still in a foul mood, Maigret telephoned the laboratory from the office in Boulevard de Courcelles.

'Moers? Getting anywhere?'

He imagined them up there, under the eaves of the Palais de Justice, working by lamplight, projecting the documents one by one on to the screen.

Moers delivered his report in a monotone, confirming

that Fumal's, Maigret's and Lucas' were the only finger-prints that had been found on all the threatening letters, with one exception. Louise Bourges' fingerprints had also been found on the first note.

This seemed to corroborate her account of events, since she claimed to have opened the first letter but not the fol-lowing ones.

But it didn't prove anything either because, if she had written the notes, she was clever enough to have done so wearing gloves.

'What about the handwriting?'

'We're still working on it. The block capitals make it tricky. So far there's nothing to indicate that Fumal didn't write the letters himself.'

The staff were still being questioned in the next room, first in groups and then separately. Pages and pages of statements had already been produced, which Maigret started leafing through.

The chauffeur Félix backed up Louise Bourges' testi-mony. He was a short, sturdy man, black-haired, with a hint of arrogance in his expression.

> *Question*: Are you Mademoiselle Bourges' lover?
> *Answer*: We're engaged.
> *Question*: Do you sleep with her?
> *Answer*: She can tell you that if she likes.
> *Question*: Do you spend most nights in her bedroom?
> *Answer*: If she said that, it must be true.
> *Question*: When do you plan on getting married?

Answer: As soon as possible.

Question: What are you waiting for?

Answer: Us to have enough money to get ourselves set up.

Question: What did you do before starting to work for Monsieur Fumal?

Answer: I was an apprentice butcher.

Question: How did he come to hire you?

Answer: He bought the butcher's where I worked, nothing new there – he never stopped buying them up, did he? He noticed me and asked if I could drive. I told him I did all the deliveries in the van.

Question: Was Louise Bourges already working for him?

Answer: No.

Question: Did you know her?

Answer: No.

Question: Did your boss ever walk anywhere in Paris?

Answer: He had three cars.

Question: Could he drive?

Answer: No. I went everywhere with him.

Question: Including Rue de l'Étoile?

Answer: Yes.

Question: Did you know who he was seeing there?

Answer: His piece on the side.

Question: Did you know her?

Answer: I drove them places. They sometimes went to a restaurant or Montmartre together.

Question: Fumal didn't try to shake you off recently, did he?

Answer: I don't understand.

Question: He didn't ask you to drive him somewhere, for instance, then take a taxi on to somewhere else?

Answer: Not that I noticed.

Question: Did he ever get you to stop outside a stationer's or a newsagent? Did he send you to buy writing paper?

Answer: No.

There were pages and pages of questions. At one point, he read:

Question: Do you consider him a good boss?

Answer: There's no such thing as a good boss.

Question: Did you hate him?

No answer.

Question: Did Louise Bourges have sexual relations with him?

Answer: Fumal or no Fumal, I would have smashed his face in, and if you're insinuating . . .

Question: He didn't try it on, then?

Answer: Luckily for him.

Question: Did you steal from him?

Answer: I'm sorry?

Question: I'm asking if you made anything on the side, on the petrol, say, or repairs, that sort of thing.

Answer: You obviously didn't know him.

Question: Was he tight with money?

Answer: He didn't want to be taken for an idiot.

Question: So you had nothing but your wages?

In the file for Louise Bourges, Maigret read:

> *Question*: Did your boss ever try to sleep with you?
> *Answer*: He had a girl for that.
> *Question*: Did he still have sexual relations with his wife?
> *Answer*: That's none of my business.
> *Question*: Did anyone ever give you money to influence him, say, or pass on anything he was planning to do?
> *Answer*: It was impossible to influence him, and he didn't confide his plans to anyone.
> *Question*: How much longer did you intend to work for him?
> *Answer*: The bare minimum.

Germaine, the maid responsible for the heavy cleaning in the house, was born in Saint-Fiacre, where her brother was still a tenant farmer. Fumal had bought his farm, as he had almost all the farms that belonged to the counts of Saint-Fiacre.

> *Question*: How did you come to start working for him?
> *Answer*: I was a widow. I was working at my brother's. Monsieur Fumal suggested I come to Paris.
> *Question*: Have you been happy here?
> *Answer*: When have I ever been happy?
> *Question*: Did you like your boss?
> *Answer*: He didn't like anyone.
> *Question*: But did you?
> *Answer*: I don't have time to ask myself questions.

Question: Did you know that Madame Fumal's brother often came and slept on the second floor?

Answer: That's no concern of mine.

Question: Did it ever occur to you to talk to your boss about it?

Answer: The boss's carrying on is none of my business.

Question: Are you planning on continuing to work for Madame Fumal?

Answer: I'll do what I've done all my life. I'll go where I'm wanted.

The telephone rang on the desk. Maigret picked up. It was Rue de Maistre station in Montmartre.

'The guy you're looking for is here.'

'Which guy?'

'Émile Lentin. They found him in a bistro near Place Clichy.'

'Is he drunk?'

'Getting there.'

'What does he have to say for himself?'

'Nothing.'

'Take him to Quai des Orfèvres. I'll be there in a little while.'

Still no sign of a gun in the house or the outbuildings.

Monsieur Joseph was sitting on one of the uncomfortable Renaissance armchairs on the landing, biting his nails as he waited to be questioned for the third time.

6. The Man in the Box Room and the Borrowings from Petty Cash

It was five o'clock when Maigret got to Quai des Orfèvres, where the lights were on. That made it one more day without a glimpse of sun. You wouldn't even have suspected such a thing still existed behind the thick, malevolent-looking layer of cloud.

Various messages, as usual, were waiting for him on his desk, most of them concerning Mrs Britt. The public never gets going immediately. It's as if they're suspicious of cases the press has only just started to talk about. But after two or three days Paris begins to bear fruit, then the regions. The story of the missing Englishwoman had already reached the remotest villages, even overseas.

One of the messages was from Monte-Carlo, where she'd supposedly been seen at a gaming table by two people, one of whom was a croupier. As this wasn't entirely unlikely, Maigret went into the inspectors' office to give the relevant instructions.

The office was almost empty.

'They've brought someone for you, chief. Seeing the state of him, I thought it best to lock him in the box room.'

That was their name for a narrow room at the end of the corridor, which had the advantage of only being lit by an unreachable skylight. After a suspect had thrown himself out of the window of the office where he had been put while they waited to question him, a grey-painted bench had been moved into the former storeroom and a sturdy lock fitted to its door.

'How is he?'

'Drunk. He's lying flat on his back, fast asleep. I hope he hasn't thrown up.'

Maigret had spent the taxi ride back from Boulevard de Courcelles thinking about Fumal and the strange way he had died.

He was a very suspicious man, all the testimony agreed on that. An innocent is the last thing he was. And he was obviously quite a shrewd judge of people, you had to grant him that.

He hadn't been killed in his bed or caught off guard in any way.

He had been found fully dressed, in his office. He had been standing in front of a cabinet containing files when he was shot at point-blank range from behind.

Had the murderer been able to silently enter the room and get within shooting range without arousing his suspicions? Unlikely, given that the parquet floor in his office was largely uncarpeted.

So Fumal must have known him, been aware he was behind him and had no inkling he was going to be attacked.

Maigret had glanced over the papers in the mahogany cabinet, which were a complete mystery to him, mainly business papers, contracts, deeds of sale or transfer. He had sent for a specialist from the finance department, who had arrived and was going through them one by one.

In another cabinet, two packs of writing paper of the kind used for the anonymous notes had been found, which meant more work for the police. First Moers was going to try to find out who the manufacturer was, then the inspectors would question all the shop managers who sold paper of that sort.

'The commissioner hasn't asked for me, has he?'

'No, chief.'

What was the point of going to see him now? To tell him he hadn't found anything? He had been given the job of looking after Fumal's life, and a few hours later Fumal was dead. Was the minister furious? Or was he actually secretly relieved?

'Have you got the key?'

The key to the box room, in other words. He headed to the end of the corridor, listened through the door for a moment. Hearing nothing, he opened it and saw an extremely lanky-looking man stretched out on the bench with his head resting on his folded arms.

While not actually a tramp's, his suit was old, crumpled, stained, like that of someone who sleeps fully dressed wherever he finds himself. His brown hair was too long, especially at the back.

Maigret touched his shoulder, then shook him until the drunkard stirred, groaning, and finally turned over almost completely.

'What is it?' he grunted, slurring his words.

'Do you want a glass of water?'

Émile Lentin sat up, still not knowing where he was, opened his eyes and looked at Maigret for a long time, wondering why this man was standing in front of him.

'Don't you remember? You're at the Police Judiciaire. I am Detective Chief Inspector Maigret.'

Gradually he came to, and the expression on his face changed, became fearful, sly.

'Why have I been brought here?'

'Can you understand what I'm saying to you?'

He ran his tongue over his dry lips.

'I'm thirsty.'

'Come to my office.'

He let him go first. Lentin's legs were too weak for there to be any danger of him running away.

'Have a drink of this, at least.'

Maigret handed him a large glass of water and two aspirin tablets, which Madame Fumal's brother swallowed meekly.

His face was ravaged, his eyelids reddish, his watery eyes almost brimming over.

'I haven't done anything,' he began, before Maigret could speak. 'Jeanne hasn't done anything either.'

'Sit down.'

He perched tentatively on the edge of a chair.

'How long have you known your brother-in-law was dead?'

The man stared at him without answering, so Maigret went on:

'When they tracked you down in Montmartre the newspapers hadn't come out yet. Did the police tell you about it?'

He struggled to remember, repeating:

'The police?'

'The police who picked you up in the bar.'

He tried to smile politely.

'Perhaps . . . Yes . . . There was something like that . . . I'm sorry . . .'

'How long have you been drunk?'

'I don't know . . . A long time . . .'

'But you knew Fumal was dead?'

'I knew that it would turn out like this.'

'That what would turn out like this?'

'That it would all be pinned on me.'

'Did you sleep at Boulevard de Courcelles?'

It was clearly a struggle for him to follow Maigret's, and his own, train of thought. He must have had a terrible hangover, and his forehead was beaded with sweat.

'I don't suppose you'd give me anything to drink? Not much . . . You know, just something to pick me up . . .'

It was true that in his condition a small glass of alcohol would be steadying, for a while at least. He'd reached the same stage in his drinking as hardened junkies who go through agony when it's time for their fix.

Maigret opened his cupboard and poured a little cognac in a glass while Lentin watched him with stunned gratitude. It must have been the first time in his life that the police had given him anything to drink.

'Now, you're going to try and give detailed answers to my questions.'

'Cross my heart!' he said, already sitting more comfortably in his chair.

'You spent the night, or part of the night, in your sister's apartment, as you often do.'

'Whenever I'm in the neighbourhood.'

'What time did you leave Boulevard de Courcelles?'

He looked intently at Maigret again, seemingly in two minds, struggling to weigh up the pros and cons.

'I suppose I'd better tell the truth?'

'Correct.'

'It was a little after one in the morning, maybe two. I had gone there in the late afternoon. I went to sleep on the couch because I was very tired.'

'Were you drunk?'

'Maybe. I'd definitely been drinking.'

'Then what happened?'

'At some point, Jeanne, my sister, brought me something to eat, some cold chicken. She hardly ever has her meals with her husband. They take up her lunch and dinner on a tray. When I'm there, she usually asks for cold cuts – ham, chicken, things like that – and shares them with me.'

'Do you know what time it was?'

'No. I haven't had a watch for ages.'

'Did you and your sister chat?'

'What would we have said to each other?'

That was one of the most tragic things Maigret had ever heard. Exactly what would they have had to say to each other? They were both almost equally far gone. They were long past the point where people still go over old memories, vent their grievances.

'I asked her for a drink.'

'How did your sister get alcohol? Did her husband keep her stocked up?'

'He never gave her enough. I'd go and buy it for her.'

'Did she have money?'

He sighed and looked at the cupboard. Maigret didn't offer him another glass.

'It's so complicated . . .'

'What's complicated?'

'Everything . . . That whole set-up . . . I knew people wouldn't understand and that's why I left . . .'

'Wait a moment, Lentin. Let's take it one step at a time. Your sister brought you some food. You asked her for a drink. You don't know what time it was, but it was already dark, is that right?'

'Definitely.'

'Did you have a drink together?'

'Only one or two. She wasn't feeling well. She has trouble breathing sometimes. She went to bed.'

'Then what?'

'I lay on the couch and smoked some cigarettes. I wondered what time it was. I listened to the sounds from the boulevard, where only the odd car went past. Without putting on my shoes, I went out on to the landing and saw the house was dark.'

'What were you intending to do?'

'I didn't have a sou. Not even a ten-franc coin. Jeanne didn't have any money either. Fumal didn't give her any, and she often had to borrow from the maids.'

'Did you want to ask your brother-in-law for money?'

He almost laughed.

'Of course not! All right, I've got to make a clean breast of it all . . . Here you go! Has anyone told you how suspicious he was? He didn't trust a soul, that man. Every bit of furniture in the house was locked. But I'd made a discovery. His secretary, Mademoiselle Louise, always kept some money in her drawer. Not much. Never more than five or six thousand francs, mainly in change and small notes, for buying stamps, sending letters by registered post, giving tips. Petty cash, they called it.

'So from time to time when I was cleaned out, I'd go down to the office and take a few hundred franc coins . . .'

'Fumal never caught you?'

'No. If I could I'd pick a night when he was out. But once or twice he'd gone to sleep and he didn't hear anything. I walk like a cat.'

'Wasn't he asleep yesterday?'

'Not in his bed, at least.'

'What did he say to you?'

'He didn't say anything to me for the very good reason that he was dead, stretched out full length on the carpet.'

'Did you take some money anyway?'

'I almost took his wallet. There, I'm being straight with you, aren't I? I thought I'd be accused, sooner or later, and that it'd be a good while before I could go back to the house.'

'Were there any lights on in the office?'

'If there had been I would have seen them under the door and I wouldn't have gone in.'

'Did you turn on the switch?'

'No. I had a torch.'

'What did you touch?'

'I touched his hand first, which was cold. So he was dead. Then I opened the drawer of his secretary's desk.'

'Were you wearing gloves?'

'No.'

It would be easy to check. The specialists had gone over both offices for fingerprints and were sorting through them upstairs. If Lentin was telling the truth they would find his prints on Mademoiselle Bourges' desk.

'You didn't see the revolver?'

'No. My first thought was to leave without telling my sister. Then I thought I'd better let her know, so I went back upstairs. I woke her up and said:

' "Your husband is dead . . . " '

'She didn't believe me. She went downstairs with me, in her nightie, and I shone my torch on the body while she looked in from the door.'

'Did she touch anything?'

'She didn't even go into the room. She said:

' "It's true, he does look dead. Finally!" '

That would explain her lack of reaction when Maigret had told her about Fumal's death that morning.

'Then what?'

'We went back upstairs and had a drink.'

'To celebrate?'

'More or less. After a while we were very merry, the two of us, and I'm pretty sure we started laughing. I can't remember if it was her or me who said:

' "Dad hanged himself too soon . . ." '

'Didn't it occur to you to tell the police?'

Lentin looked at him, dumbfounded. Why would they have told the police? Fumal was dead. That was all that mattered, as far as they were concerned.

'In the end I thought I'd better clear out. If I was found in the house . . .'

'What time was it?'

'I don't know. I walked to Place Clichy, and almost all the bars were shut. In fact, I think only one was open. I had a drink or two. Then I walked the boulevards to Pigalle, went into another bar and, in the end, I must have fallen asleep somewhere on a banquette, but I don't know where. I was thrown out at daybreak and walked some more. I did come and have a look at the house from Boulevard des Batignolles, though.'

'Why?'

'To see what was happening. There were some cars outside and a policeman at the door. I didn't go any nearer. I carried on walking . . .'

That word recurred like a leitmotiv, and it was true, walking, like propping up a bar, was one of Lentin's main occupations.

'Don't you ever work?'

'Sometimes I muck in at Les Halles or on a building site.'

He must have opened car doors outside hotels as well, maybe done some petty shoplifting. Maigret would get Records upstairs to check if he had any convictions.

'Do you have a revolver?'

'If I had one I would have sold it a long time ago. And

the police would have taken it off me a long time ago too, because I've given up counting the number of times they've brought me in and kept me overnight in the station.'

'What about your sister?'

'What about her?'

'Does she have a gun?'

'You don't know her. I'm tired, detective chief inspector. I've been nice, come on, admit it; I've told you everything I know. If you'd only just give me another little drop . . .'

His gaze was humble, beseeching.

'Just a tiny little drop!' he repeated.

There was probably nothing more to be got out of him, and Maigret headed to the cupboard. Lentin's face lit up.

Maigret suddenly switched to the familiar 'tu', as he had with Martine Gilloux:

'Don't you miss your wife and kids?'

The man hesitated, glass in hand, then drained it in one go and muttered reproachfully:

'What are you bringing that up for? The kids are grown up, for a start. Two of them are married, and they wouldn't give me a second look if they passed me in the street.'

'Don't you know who killed Fumal?'

'If I knew, I'd go and say thank you. And if I'd had the guts, I would have done it myself. I'd sworn to when my father died. I told my sister. She said that the only thing that would come of it was that I'd spend the rest of my days in jail. Still, if I'd found a way to do it without getting caught . . .'

Had the man or woman who'd actually killed Fumal thought the same, waited for the chance to act safely?

'Have you got any other questions for me?'

No. Maigret couldn't think of anything else to ask him. He just said:

'What are you going to do if I let you go?'

Lentin made a vague gesture encompassing the city which he would vanish back into.

'I'm going to keep you in for a day or two.'

'Without anything to drink?'

'You'll get a glass of wine tomorrow morning. You need to rest.'

The bench in the box room was hard. Maigret rang for an inspector.

'Take him to the cells. Tell them to make sure he eats and sleeps.'

As he got up the man took a last look at the cupboard. He opened his mouth to ask again but didn't dare. Instead he went out, stammering:

'Thank you.'

Maigret called the inspector back.

'Have his prints taken and give them to Moers.'

He added a brief explanation, while Madame Fumal's brother stood vacantly in the middle of the deserted corridor, making no attempt to get away.

Maigret remained sitting at his desk for ten long minutes, staring straight ahead, smoking his pipe as if in a reverie. Finally, he peeled himself off his chair and headed towards the inspectors' room. It was still almost empty. A murmur of voices could be heard in the next office. He went in and found everyone gathered there who had spent the day working in the Boulevard de Courcelles townhouse.

Only one man had been left on the premises, Inspector Neveu, who was going to be relieved at any moment.

As per Maigret's orders, the officers were comparing the answers they had been given in the different interrogations.

Almost everybody had been questioned two or three times. Monsieur Joseph had been called back five times, returning after each session to wait on the landing with the Renaissance chairs and the two marble statues.

'I suppose I have the right to go out and attend to my affairs?' he had asked finally.

'No.'

'Not even to eat?'

'There's a cook in the house.'

The kitchen was on the ground floor, behind Victor's lodge. The cook was a fat, middle-aged woman, a widow, who seemed completely unaware of what went on in the house. A characteristic exchange went:

> *Question:* What do you think about Monsieur Fumal?
> *Answer:* What do you expect me to think? Do I know him?
> She points to the dumbwaiter, her kitchen ceiling.
> *Answer:* I work down here and he eats up there.
> *Question:* Doesn't he ever come down to see you?
> *Answer:* He sends for me now and then to give me instructions and also, once a month, so I can give him my accounts.

Question: Was he careful with money?
Answer: What do you mean by careful with money?

Asked about Louise Bourges, she said:

Answer: Sleeping with someone is what you do at that age. Those days are over for me, more's the pity!

Her view on Madame Fumal:

Answer: It takes all sorts.

How long had she been in the house?

Answer: Three months.
Question: Did you think there was a strange atmosphere?
Answer: If you'd seen what I've seen in well-to-do houses!
It is true that she has had dozens of different jobs in her life.
Question: Haven't you felt at home anywhere?
Answer: I like change, I do.

Every few months she would reappear in the waiting area of the job exchange, where she was a sort of honorary member. She specialized in temporary cover and jobs for foreigners passing through Paris.

Question: Didn't you see or hear anything?
Answer: When I sleep, I sleep.

Maigret had set his men the meticulous task they were sweating over because he still hoped that some revealing contradiction between different testimonies might come to light, even if only on a point of detail.

If Roger Gaillardin wasn't the murderer – and it was more or less certain that he wasn't – Fumal hadn't been killed by an outsider.

Inspector Vacher, who had been watching the townhouse all evening, confirmed Victor's account, almost to the minute.

So, shortly before eight o'clock, Fumal's car had driven back into the courtyard. Félix, the chauffeur, was at the wheel. Fumal and his secretary were in the back.

Victor had closed the carriage gate behind them, and it hadn't been opened again that night.

Victor went on to say that Louise Bourges had gone up to the first floor with her employer but had only stayed there for a few minutes and had then gone to the staff dining room next to the kitchen.

She ate her evening meal there. Germaine, the chambermaid, went up to serve Fumal while Noémi took a tray up to the second floor for Madame Fumal.

All this seemed well attested. Nothing in the testimonies suggested otherwise.

After dinner Louise Bourges had gone back up to the office, where she had stayed roughly half an hour. Around 9.30 she had crossed the courtyard and entered the staff quarters.

When questioned, Félix said:

Answer: I went up to her room, as I did most nights.

Question: Why did you sleep in her room and not yours?

Answer: Because hers is bigger.

Louise Bourges had unblushingly said the same. Germaine, the chambermaid, took up the story:

Answer: I heard them at it for at least an hour. To look at, she seems a cold fish. But if you had to sleep next door to her with only a partition between you and her bed . . .

Question: What time did you go to sleep?

Answer: I wound up the alarm clock at ten thirty.

Question: Did you hear anything during the night?

Answer: No.

Question: Did you know about Émile Lentin's visits to his sister?

Answer: Everybody does.

Question: Who do you mean by everybody?

Answer: Noémi, the cook . . .

Question: How did the cook, who never goes up to the second floor, know?

Answer: Because I told her.

Question: Why?

Answer: So she'd give them double servings when he was there, of course!

Question: Did Victor know too?

Answer: I didn't say anything to him about it. I've never trusted him. But he's not the type of person you can hide things from.

Question: And the secretary?

Answer: Félix is bound to have told her.

Question: And how did Félix know?

Answer: Through Noémi.

So everyone in the house knew that Lentin regularly slept in the little room on the second floor – everyone, that is, except possibly Ferdinand Fumal . . .

. . . and Monsieur Joseph, who slept in the room directly overhead:

Question: Do you know Émile Lentin?

Answer: I did before he started drinking.

Question: Did his brother-in-law ruin him?

Answer: People who ruin themselves always blame other people.

Question: Do you mean he was reckless?

Answer: He thought he was smarter than he was.

Question: And he found himself up against someone really smart?

Answer: If you like. That's business.

Question: Did he then try to borrow money from his brother-in-law?

Answer: Probably.

Question: Without luck?

Answer: Even if you're very rich you can't help all of life's failures.

Question: Did you see him at Boulevard de Courcelles?

Answer: Years ago.

Question: Where?

Answer: In Monsieur Fumal's office.

Question: What happened between them?

Answer: Monsieur Fumal threw him out.

Question: Have you seen him since?

Answer: Once, in the street, near Châtelet. He was drunk.

Question: Did he talk to you?

Answer: He told me to tell his brother-in-law that he was a bastard.

Question: Did you know that he sometimes slept in the house?

Answer: No.

Question: If you had known, would you have told your boss?

Answer: Probably.

Question: You're not sure.

Answer: I haven't thought about it.

Question: No one told you?

Answer: People don't talk to me if they have a choice.

This was true. It tallied with the maids' accounts. Noémi summed up the general feeling about Monsieur Joseph when she said:

> *Answer:* He moved around the house like a mouse behind the wainscots. You never knew when he was coming or going. You didn't even know exactly what he was doing.

The statements tallied about the rest of the night too. Monsieur Joseph had rung the bell just after 9.30. The little door in the carriage gate had opened and closed behind him.

Question: Why didn't you come in by the back door when you had a key?

Answer: I only used that door when it was late or when I was going straight up to my apartment.

Question: Did you stop on the first floor?

Answer: Yes. As I've said three times.

Question: Was Monsieur Fumal alive?

Answer: Same as you and me.

Question: What did you talk about?

Answer: Business.

Question: Was there anyone else in the office?

Answer: No.

Question: Did Fumal tell you he was expecting a visit?

Answer: Yes.

Question: Why didn't you say so earlier?

Answer: Because you didn't ask me. He was expecting Gaillardin and knew why he was coming. Gaillardin was still hoping for an extension. We decided not to give him one.

Question: Didn't you stay for the conversation?

Answer: No.

Question: Why?

Answer: Because I don't like firing squads.

Amazingly, that seemed to be true. Looking at the fellow, you felt he was capable of every crooked scheme, every base act, but only, it seemed, so long as he didn't have to look a person in the eye and tell him his fate.

Question: Did you hear Gaillardin arrive from upstairs?

Answer: You can't hear anything in the house from up there. Have a try!

Question: Weren't you curious enough to go down afterwards to find out what had happened?

Answer: I already knew.

Immediately realizing the ambiguity of his answer, he corrected himself:

Answer: I mean, I knew that Monsieur Fumal would say no, that Gaillardin would plead with him, talk about his wife, his children, as they all do, even when they're living with their mistress, but that it wouldn't get him anywhere.

Question: Do you think that he killed Fumal?

Answer: I've already said what I thought.

Question: Had you and your boss argued recently?

Answer: We never argued.

Question: How much are you paid, Monsieur Goldman?

Answer: Have a look at my tax returns.

Question: That's not an answer.

Answer: You can't get a better answer.

No one, at all events, had seen him come back downstairs. Although it was true that no one had seen or heard Émile Lentin go downstairs either, on his own first and then with his sister, and then eventually leave by the little door on Rue de Prony.

A few minutes before ten, a taxi had stopped on the boulevard. Gaillardin had got out, paid the driver and rung the bell.

121

Exactly seventeen minutes later, Inspector Vacher had seen him come back out and walk off towards l'Étoile, occasionally looking over his shoulder to see if a taxi was coming.

Vacher hadn't been able to watch the little back door, because he didn't know it existed.

Wasn't that Maigret's fault, because he hadn't believed the anonymous letters and only grudgingly had the house watched?

The office was thick with pipe and cigarette smoke.

Every now and then, the inspectors swapped pieces of paper marked up in red and blue pencil.

'What would you say to a glass of beer, boys?'

Hours of poring over every sentence in the transcripts still lay ahead of them. Later they'd have sandwiches sent up.

The telephone rang. Someone picked up.

'For you, chief.'

It was Moers, who had finished with the fingerprints and confirmed that Lentin's prints had only been found on the door handle and the drawer of the secretary's desk.

'Someone's got to be lying!' Maigret shouted angrily.

Unless there wasn't a murderer at all, which was impossible.

7. A Simple Maths Problem and a Less Innocent Souvenir of the War

Maigret felt a sense of relief as profound and luxuriant as, for instance, when you have a hot bath after spending three days and nights on a train.

He knew that he was asleep, that he was in his own bed, that he only had to reach out a hand to touch his wife's hip. He even knew that it was the middle of the night, around two o'clock at the latest.

But he was dreaming. Don't you sometimes have intuitions when you're dreaming that you wouldn't if you were awake? Can't the mind sometimes grow more rather than less acute while you're asleep?

It had certainly happened to him once, when he was a student. He had sweated over a difficult problem all evening, and then suddenly the answer had come to him in a dream in the middle of the night. When he had woken up he hadn't remembered it immediately, but he had got there in the end.

The same thing was happening now. If his wife had turned on the light, no doubt she would have seen a mocking smile on his face.

He was laughing at himself. He had made too much of a tragedy out of Fumal's case. He had rushed in headlong and been completely in the dark.

Was he still scared, at his age, of a minister who might be gone in a week or a month?

He had got off on the wrong foot. He'd known that immediately, from the moment Boom-Boom had come to see him in his office. But instead of getting a grip, quietly smoking a pipe and having a glass of beer to calm his nerves, he had plunged ahead.

Now he'd found the solution, as he had with his old problem.

It had come to him a bit like an air bubble rising to the surface of water. At last he could relax.

All over! Tomorrow morning, he would set the wheels in motion and that would be that for the Fumal case. Then all he'd have to do was take care of the irksome Mrs Britt and find her, dead or alive.

The main thing was not to forget his discovery. He had to get it straight in his mind first, register it as something more than a faint glimmer. He knew what that meant: one or two sentences. Brevity is the mark of truth. Who had said that? Didn't matter. One sentence. Then wake up and . . .

He opened his eyes suddenly in the dark bedroom and frowned. His dream wasn't entirely over, though; the truth still felt within his grasp.

His wife was sleeping, all warm, and he lay on his back so he could think more easily.

It was something very simple to which he hadn't paid sufficient attention during the day. He had laughed when he realized it in his dream. Why?

He tried to recover his train of thought. It was about

someone he'd been in contact with several times, he was sure.

An insignificant fact. Was it actually a fact? Was it a physical clue?

An almost painful tension replaced his relaxed, dreamy state. He forced himself to concentrate, desperately trying to visualize the mansion on Boulevard de Courcelles from top to bottom, its occupants, everyone who had visited it.

He and his inspectors had worked on the witness statements at Quai des Orfèvres until ten at night. By the end, they had known every slightest reply off by heart, like some old refrain.

Was it something in those transcripts? Was it to do with Louise Bourges and Félix?

He was tempted to think so, started searching along those lines. After all, there was nothing to prove it wasn't the secretary who had written the anonymous notes.

Maigret hadn't asked her how much she earned at Fumal's. Still, she can't have been paid more than the going rate for a secretary.

She was Félix's mistress, she was very open about that, but she was quick to add:

'We're engaged too.'

The chauffeur said the same.

'When do you plan on getting married?'

'When we've put aside enough money to buy an inn in Gien.'

No one says they're engaged if they're planning to get married in ten or fifteen years.

Maigret did a few sums in bed. Supposing that Louise

and Félix spent the bare minimum on clothes and incidental expenses, or even saved their entire wages, it would still take them at least ten years to buy a business, however small.

This wasn't what he'd hit on in his sleep just now, but it was worth bearing in mind.

One of them must have had a faster way of making money, and since they were still at Boulevard de Courcelles, despite loathing it, Fumal must have been involved somehow.

Fumal had humiliated his secretary, treated her in the most squalid way imaginable.

She hadn't said anything about it to Maigret or the inspectors.

Had she confessed it to Félix? Had he stayed calm when he heard that his mistress had been made to undress, contemptuously felt up, and then, when she was stark naked, told to put her clothes on again?

That wasn't it either. It was along those lines, but more revealing.

Maigret was tempted to go back to sleep to try to recapture his dream but he couldn't sleep now, his brain was whirring like the cogs in a clock.

There was something else, more recent . . .

He almost gritted his teeth in an effort to remember, to concentrate. Suddenly he saw Émile Lentin in his office again and thought he could hear his voice. What had Lentin said that was connected to Louise Bourges? He hadn't talked directly about her, but about something to do with her.

He had confessed . . . That was it!

Maigret was getting somewhere after all. Émile Lentin had said he sometimes used to creep down to the office in his socks to take money out of the petty cash – a few hundred-franc coins at a time, he had said.

So, that money was in Louise's drawer. It was her responsibility. She probably recorded her expenses in a notebook, in the normal way.

According to Lentin, these thefts were frequent.

And yet she had never mentioned them. Was it believable that she hadn't spotted anything, hadn't noticed her accounts were wrong?

So there were two things about which she had, if not lied, then certainly kept quiet.

Why hadn't she been worried when she found money missing from her drawer?

Was it because she took some herself, and her accounts were fiddled as it was?

Or because she knew who was committing the thefts and had reasons not to say anything?

He felt the urge to smoke a pipe and noiselessly got out of bed, taking almost two minutes to slip out from under the sheets and pad over to the chest of drawers.

Madame Maigret stirred, sighed, but didn't wake up. Cupping the match in his hand, he only let it flare up for a second.

Sitting in the wing chair, he continued to rack his brains.

He might not have found the answer in his dream, but he had still made progress. Where was he? The thefts from the drawer. If Louise Bourges knew who was breaking into the office at night . . .

He cast his mind back to that office where he had spent part of the day. Two big windows looked on to the courtyard. Across the courtyard stood the former stables and above them, not just two or three servants' rooms, as you find in certain townhouses, but two entire floors of servants' quarters, forming a small townhouse in themselves.

He had inspected the rooms there. The secretary's bedroom, where Félix used to spend the night with her, was on the second floor on the right, directly opposite the office but slightly higher up.

He tried to remember the wording of the initial reports, particularly Lapointe's, who was first on the scene. Was there any talk of the curtains?

The windows, which Maigret could picture clearly, had muslin drapes which softened the daylight but wouldn't be enough at night to hide what was happening in the lighted room.

There were also thick, Empire red curtains. Had they been open or closed when Lapointe had got there?

Maigret almost rang him at home to ask him that question, which suddenly seemed vital. If those curtains weren't closed, Louise and Félix would know everything that went on in the office.

Did that get him anywhere?

Should he conclude that they had witnessed the previous night's drama from their room and knew who the murderer was?

There was a safe over a metre tall in a corner of the office that he wouldn't be able to examine until the following day. It could only be opened in the presence of an examining magistrate and lawyer.

What did Fumal keep in that safe? They hadn't found a will among his papers. They had rung the lawyer, Maitre Audoin, who had no knowledge of one either.

Motionless in the dark, Maigret kept mining this seam, although he sensed he wasn't quite on the right track yet. The revelation he'd had moments ago, in the dream, was more complete, blindingly obvious.

Lentin had frequently gone down to the office, sometimes when Fumal was asleep in his bedroom . . .

That could open up new avenues. Admittedly there was a room between the office and the bedroom that would muffle sound, but Fumal was someone who distrusted everybody, and with good reason.

Lentin's thefts had gone on for years. Wasn't it conceivable that on one or more occasions the former butcher had heard a noise?

He was a physical coward, Maigret knew. He'd been one when they were still at school, playing mean tricks on classmates and when they turned on him, moaning, 'Don't hit me!'

Or, more often, he would go and place himself under the protection of the teacher.

Supposing that, a fortnight or so before, Lentin had gone to commit one of his petty thefts . . .

Supposing Fumal had heard some noise . . .

Maigret imagined the king of the meat trade clenching

his revolver in his hand, not daring to go and see what was happening.

If he didn't know his brother-in-law was in the house, which he might easily not have, he must have thought it could be anybody, including Monsieur Joseph and his secretary, maybe even his wife.

Had he thought they were after the petty cash? You would almost need second sight to do that.

Why would a stranger be going into his office? Wasn't that person going to open his bedroom door? These sorts of questions must have been running through his mind.

That made sense. It wasn't the dream yet but it was another step forwards. In fact, it might explain why Fumal had started writing anonymous letters to give himself an excuse to go to the police.

He could have gone to the police anyway. But that would have meant acknowledging the fear he was living in.

Madame Maigret stirred, pushed back the blanket, suddenly exclaimed:

'Where are you?'

From the depths of his armchair, he said:

'Here.'

'What are you doing?'

'I'm smoking a pipe. I couldn't sleep.'

'Haven't you gone to bed yet? What time is it?'

He turned on the light. The alarm clock showed 3.10. He emptied his pipe, went back to bed feeling dissatisfied, hoping without much conviction to recover the thread of his dream, and when he woke up he was greeted by the smell of fresh coffee. He was startled to see the sun, a genuine swathe of sunshine falling into the bedroom for the first time in at least two weeks.

'You weren't sleepwalking last night, were you?'

'No.'

'Do you remember sitting in the dark, smoking your pipe?'

'Yes.'

He remembered everything, all his reasoning, but not the dream, unfortunately. He got dressed, had breakfast, walked to Place de la République, bought the morning papers at a newspaper stand and caught the bus.

The faces around him were cheerful, thanks to the sun. The air had already lost its aftertaste of damp and dust. The sky was pale blue. The pavements and roofs were dry, and only the tree trunks were still wet.

Fumal, King of Meat Trade . . .

The morning papers repeated the previous evening's stories with further details and new photographs, including one of Maigret coming out of the mansion on Boulevard de Courcelles with his hat pulled down over his eyes, looking morose.

One of the sub-headings struck him:

On day of death, Fumal 'asks for police protection'

There had been a leak somewhere. The ministry, where any number of people must have known about the butcher's telephone call? Or Louise Bourges, who had been questioned by the journalists?

Of course, one of his inspectors could always have inadvertently been indiscreet too.

A few hours before his tragic death, Ferdinand Fumal went to Quai des Orfèvres, where he is alleged to have informed Detective Chief Inspector Maigret of serious threats against his life. We understand that at the very moment he was killed in his office, an inspector from the Police Judiciaire was on guard in Boulevard de Courcelles.

There was no mention of the minister, but the implication was that Fumal had acquired tremendous political influence.

He slowly climbed the main staircase and waved good morning to Joseph, fully expecting to hear him say the big boss wanted to see him, but Joseph didn't bat an eyelid.

Some reports were waiting for him on his desk, which he merely glanced at.

The forensic doctor's report confirmed what he already knew. Fumal had been shot at point-blank range. The firearm had been less than twenty centimetres from his body when it was fired. The bullet had been found in the ribcage.

The weapons expert who examined the bullet had been equally categorical. It had been fired from a Luger automatic of the sort German officers carried in the last war.

A telegram concerning Mrs Britt had arrived from Monte-Carlo: the woman spotted at the tables wasn't her but a Dutch woman who looked very similar.

The briefing bell rang in the corridor, and he headed, sighing, to the commissioner's office where he distractedly shook hands with his assembled colleagues.

As he had expected, he was the centre of attention. They of all people knew what a tricky situation he was in and they had a discreet way of showing their sympathy.

As for the commissioner, he pretended to take it lightly, optimistically.

'Nothing new, Maigret?'

'The investigation is proceeding.'

'Have you read the papers?'

'I've just had a look at them now. They'll only be satisfied when I arrest somebody.'

The press was going to hound him. This business, on top of the Englishwoman vanishing into thin air in the middle of Paris, was doing nothing for the Police Judiciaire's prestige.

'I'm doing my best,' he sighed again.

'Any leads?'

He shrugged. Could you call them leads?

Everyone then talked about their particular cases, and there was something like commiseration in the looks they gave Maigret when the meeting broke up.

The expert from the finance department was waiting for him in his office. Maigret listened with half an ear, still trying to recapture his dream.

Fumal's business interests were far more extensive than the newspapers imagined. In a matter of years, he had built up a virtual monopoly of the meat trade.

'There's someone fiendishly intelligent behind these transactions,' explained the expert, 'someone who is very knowledgeable about the law. It will take months to unravel the web of companies and subsidiaries leading back to Fumal. The Inland Revenue will certainly be looking into all this from their end.'

Monsieur Joseph was probably the brains he was referring to, because, although Fumal had amassed an impressive fortune before they met, he had never done business on such a scale.

The finance department of the prosecutor's office could investigate all they wanted, the Inland Revenue too, for all he cared.

What he was interested in was finding out who had shot Fumal at point-blank range in his office while Vacher was pacing up and down on the pavement.

He was wanted on the telephone; apparently someone insisted on talking to him personally. It turned out to be Madame Gaillardin, the real one, the wife in Neuilly, who was calling from Cannes, where she still was with her children. She was full of questions. A Côte d'Azur newspaper, she said, had reported that, after killing Fumal at Boulevard de Courcelles, Gaillardin had gone to Puteaux and committed suicide.

'I rang my lawyer this morning. I'm getting the Mistral in a moment. I want you to know, as of now, that the woman at Rue François Premier has no rights, that there was never any question of my husband and I getting a divorce, and that we were married under the convention of common assets. Fumal swindled him, there's absolutely no doubt about that. My lawyer will prove it and claim the amount from his estate that . . .'

Maigret sighed, holding the receiver to his ear, muttering from time to time:

'Yes, madame . . . Fine, madame . . .'

Finally, he asked:

'Tell me, did your husband have a Luger?'

'A what?'

'Nothing. Did he fight in the last war?'

'He was exempted because of . . .'

'The grounds are irrelevant. Was he a prisoner or deported to Germany?'

'No. Why?'

'No reason. Did you ever see a revolver in your apartment at Neuilly?'

'There used to be one, but he took it to the apartment of that . . . that . . .'

'Thank you.'

There was a woman who wasn't going to let herself be pushed around. She'd fight like a lioness defending her cubs.

He went into the inspectors' office and looked around for someone.

'Isn't Lapointe here?'

'He must be in the lavatory.'

He waited.

'Is Aillevard still off work?'

Lapointe finally reappeared and blushed when he found Maigret waiting for him.

'Tell me, son . . . Yesterday morning, when you went into the office . . . Think carefully . . . Were the curtains open or closed?'

'They were as you found them. I didn't touch them and I didn't see anyone touching them.'

'So they were open?'

'Definitely. I'd swear to it. Hang on . . . Yes, they were, because I noticed the old stables across the courtyard and . . .'

'Come with me.'

He liked having someone with him on an investigation, whenever possible. On the way to the townhouse in the little black car he barely opened his mouth. At Boulevard de Courcelles he pressed the brass doorbell himself, and Victor came to open the door in the carriage gate.

Maigret noticed that he hadn't shaved, which made him look far more like a poacher than a manservant or concierge.

'Is the inspector upstairs?'

'Yes. Coffee and croissants have been taken up to him.'

'Who by?'

'Noémi.'

'Has Monsieur Joseph come down?'

'I haven't see him.'

'Mademoiselle Louise?'

'She was in the kitchen having her breakfast half an hour ago. I don't know if she's gone upstairs.'

'Félix?'

'In the garage.'

Taking a few steps forwards, Maigret saw the chauffeur, who was polishing one of the cars as if nothing had happened.

'Isn't the lawyer here?'

'I didn't even know he was coming.'

'I'm expecting the examining magistrate too. Show him up to the office.'

'Very well, detective chief inspector.'

Maigret had a question on the tip of his tongue, but it slipped his memory as he was about to ask it. Anyway, it can't have been important.

On the first floor, they found Inspector Janin, who had been on guard for the second half of the night. He hadn't shaved either and was asleep on his feet.

'Anything happened?'

'Nobody's stirred. The young lady came just now and asked if I needed her. I told her I didn't, and after a bit she left, saying she would be in her room and we could just call if we wanted her.'

'Did she go into the office?'

'Yes. She was only in there for a few seconds.'

'Did she open any drawers?'

'I don't think so. She came out holding a piece of clothing, some red knitted thing, which she hadn't had when she went in.'

Maigret remembered she was wearing a red cardigan the day before. She had probably forgotten it in one of the rooms on the first floor.

'Madame Fumal?'

'They took up her breakfast on a tray.'

'Hasn't she come down?'

'I haven't seen her.'

'Go to bed. There'll be time to write your report this evening.'

The office's red curtains still weren't drawn. Maigret told Lapointe to go and ask the maids if they usually were, then looked out of one of the windows. Directly opposite, slightly higher up, a window was open, and he could see a young blonde woman bustling about, moving her lips as if she were singing as she did some housework. It was Louise Bourges.

Struck by an idea, he looked around at the safe by the wall opposite the windows. Could it be seen from across the courtyard?

If it could . . .

The idea excited him and he went downstairs, out into the courtyard, and climbed the narrower staircase that led to the secretary's bedroom. He knocked. She called:

'Come in.'

She didn't seem surprised to see him, merely muttering: 'It's you.'

He was already familiar with the room, which was spacious and elegantly furnished, with a radio and record player console and a bedside light with an orange shade. It was the window that interested him. He leaned out of it, peering at the dim outline of the office opposite. It hadn't occurred to him to switch on the lights when he left.

'Will you go and turn on some lights over there?'

'Where?'

'In the office.'

No hint of her being frightened or surprised.

'One moment . . . Do you know what's in your employer's safe?'

She hesitated, but only briefly.

'Yes. I'd rather tell the truth . . .'

'What?'

'Some important files, for one thing; Madame Fumal's jewellery; some letters, I don't know what about, and some money.'

'A lot of money?'

'Yes. I'm sure you realize why he had to have large amounts in cash. In his kind of deals, some of the balance always has to be paid under the table, some amount he couldn't pay by cheque.'

'How much, would you say?'

'I often saw him pay two or three million in cash. He had cash in his bank safe too.'

'So there would be several million in cash in the safe?'

'Unless he took it out.'

'When?'

'I don't know.'

'Go and turn on the lights.'

'Shall I come back here afterwards?'

'Wait for me over there.'

Louise Bourges' bedroom had been searched without anything being found. No Luger, no compromising papers, no money, apart from three thousand-franc notes and a few hundred-franc coins.

139

The young woman walked across the courtyard. Maigret had the sense it was taking her a long time to get to the office on the first floor, but maybe she'd met somebody on the way.

Eventually the lights came on, and immediately every smallest detail of the room opposite became visible through the muslin drapes, including the left half of the safe.

He tried to work out where Fumal had been standing when he was killed, but it was difficult to tell exactly, because the body could have rolled.

Had the killing been visible from Louise Bourges' window? You couldn't say for sure one way or another. What was certain was that you could clearly see whoever came in or out of the office.

He crossed the courtyard in his turn, started up the stairs without seeing anyone. Louise was waiting for him on the landing.

'Did you find out what you wanted to?'

He nodded. She followed him into the office.

'You'll have noticed that you can see almost all my bedroom from here too.'

He pricked up his ears.

'Monsieur Fumal may not have always drawn his office curtains, but Félix and I had the best reason to shut our shutters – those are shutters we've got over there. We're not exhibitionists, us two.'

'So sometimes he drew his curtains and sometimes he didn't?'

'That's right. For instance, when he was working late with Monsieur Joseph, he always drew them. I used to wonder why. I suppose it was because those evenings he had to open the safe.'

'Do you think Monsieur Joseph knew the combination?'

'I doubt it.'

'What about you?'

'I know I don't.'

'Lapointe! Go up to Monsieur Joseph . . . Ask him if he knows the combination of the safe . . .'

The key to the safe had been found in the dead man's pocket. Madame Fumal, who had been questioned the day before, knew nothing about it; the lawyer claimed not to know the combination either. So they were not only expecting the examining magistrate this morning, but also an expert from the safemakers.

'You're not pregnant, are you?' he asked suddenly.

'Why do you ask me that? No. I'm not.'

They heard footsteps on the stairs. It was the man from the safe company, a tall, thin individual with a moustache, who immediately looked at the safe like a surgeon studying his next patient.

'We have to wait for the examining magistrate and the lawyer.'

'I know. I've done this before.'

Once they arrived, the lawyer requested that Madame Fumal, the heiress presumptive, be present. Lapointe, who had come down from Monsieur Joseph's apartment, went to find her.

She wasn't as drunk as the day before, just a little dazed. She must have had a shot before coming down, though, to pluck up her courage, because her breath stank.

The court clerk had installed himself behind the desk.

'I don't think there's any reason for you to be here, Mademoiselle Bourges,' said Maigret, noticing the secretary.

How he would regret saying that!

He went and chatted with Judge Planche by the window while the expert got to work. It took half an hour, after which there was a click, and they saw the heavy door swing open.

The lawyer went over and looked inside first. Maigret and the examining magistrate followed.

A few yellow, bulging envelopes of receipts and correspondence, a large proportion of which were IOUs signed by a host of different names.

A shelf full of files concerning Fumal's different businesses.

But no money, not even a solitary banknote.

Sensing someone behind him, Maigret turned around. Monsieur Joseph was standing in the doorway.

'Is it there?' he asked.

'What?'

'The fifteen million. There should be fifteen million in cash in the safe. It was there three days ago, and I'm sure Monsieur Fumal didn't take it out.'

'Do you have a key?'

'I've just told your inspector I don't.'

'Does anyone have a second key to the safe?'

'Not that I know of.'

Pacing up and down, Maigret found himself facing the window; he caught sight of Louise Bourges in her bedroom opposite. She had started singing again, as though indifferent to what was going on in the house.

8. The Window, the Safe, the Lock and the Thief

They say the longest dreams only really last a few seconds. Maigret experienced something at that moment which reminded him not of the previous night's dream, which he still hadn't remembered, but of the sense of discovery that had accompanied it, that feeling of suddenly grasping a truth after you've been puzzling over it for ages.

Later he would be capable, such was the fullness of those few moments of life, to reconstruct his every slightest thought, his every slightest sensation, and if he had been a painter he could have rendered the scene with the meticulous detail of the minor Flemish masters.

The combined electric light and sunlight gave the room an artificial appearance like a stage set, which may have been why everyone seemed to be playing a role.

Maigret remained standing by one of the two tall windows. Opposite, on the other side of the courtyard, Louise Bourges was bustling about in her room, singing to herself, her blonde hair picked out by the sun. Below, in the courtyard, Félix, in blue overalls, was aiming a rubber hose at the limousine, which he had brought out of the garage.

The court clerk was sitting in the late Ferdinand Fumal's chair, looking up expectantly, poised to take dictation. Over by the safe the lawyer, Audoin, and the examining magistrate, Planche, were looking from the steel strongbox to Maigret and back again, and the lawyer still had a file in his hand.

The safe expert had discreetly withdrawn to a corner, while Monsieur Joseph had only taken a couple of steps into the room. The door was open, and young Lapointe could be seen on the landing, lighting a cigarette.

Time seemed to be suspended for a few moments, with everyone holding their pose as if they were at the photographer's.

Maigret's gaze travelled from the window opposite to the safe, then from the safe to the door, and finally he realized his mistake. The old oak door had an enormous lock to fit a large key.

'Lapointe!' he called.

'Yes, chief.'

'Go downstairs and find Victor.'

To the surprise of the others, he added:

'Be careful!'

Lapointe didn't understand the warning either. Maigret turned to the safe man to ask him a question.

'If someone had been spying on Fumal through the lock, and they'd often seen him open the safe and studied his movements, could they have worked out the combination?'

The man looked at the door in turn, seemingly assessing the angle, measuring the distance.

'It'd be child's play for me,' he said after a while.

'And for someone who's not in the trade?'

'If they were patient . . . Follow the hand movements, count how many turns he gives each disc . . .'

They heard running downstairs, then in the courtyard, and Lapointe asking Félix:

'Have you seen Victor?'

Maigret was equally sure that he had just worked out the truth and that it was all too late. Across the courtyard Louise Bourges was leaning out of her window, and he thought he saw a thin smile on her lips.

Lapointe came back upstairs, looking stunned.

'I can't find him anywhere, chief. He's not in the lodge, or anywhere else on the ground floor. He hasn't gone upstairs either. Félix claims he heard the street door open and close a few moments ago.'

'Ring headquarters. Give them his description. Tell them to alert all the railway stations and gendarmeries and get a move on. Call the neighbouring police stations yourself . . .'

The manhunt was starting, and that was a well-worn routine. The radio cars would patrol the surrounding area in ever tighter circles. Uniformed police and plainclothes inspectors would scour the streets, go into all the bistros, question the customers.

'Do you know how he's dressed?'

Maigret and his inspectors had only ever seen him in a striped waistcoat. Monsieur Joseph reluctantly stepped in, saying:

'A navy-blue suit is the extent of his wardrobe, as far as I know.'

'What sort of hat?'

'He never wore a hat.'

When Maigret had asked Lapointe to go down and look

for Victor he hadn't yet been certain by any means. Was it intuition? Or was it the conclusion of countless hypotheses he had unwittingly been testing, of an infinite number of observations that in themselves had seemed unimportant?

He had been convinced from the outset that Fumal had been killed out of hatred, as an act of revenge.

Victor's going on the run didn't contradict this, nor, however far-fetched initially, did the fact that fifteen million had disappeared from the safe. Quite the opposite, he was inclined to think.

Victor's was a peasant's hatred, after all, and a peasant rarely forgets his self-interest, even if he is in the grip of passion.

Maigret didn't say anything. Everyone looked at him. He felt humiliated because he had failed. He had spent too long circling the truth and now had little confidence in the manhunt that was being organized.

'Gentlemen, I won't keep you. If you want to get the formalities over with . . .'

The examining magistrate, who hadn't been in the job very long, didn't dare question his decision. It was all he could do to mutter:

'Do you think it's him?'

'I'm sure of it.'

'And he took the millions?'

Most probably. Either Victor had them on him or he had hidden them somewhere and was going to fetch them.

Lapointe's monotonous voice was repeating the

description into the telephone as Maigret trudged down to the courtyard. He looked at Félix, who was still washing the car, for a moment.

Then he walked past him without a word, climbed the stairs and pushed open the door to Louise Bourges' bedroom.

There was a glint of mischief and profound satisfaction in her eyes.

'Did you know?' he simply said.

She didn't try to deny it, retorting instead:

'Admit it, you suspected me, didn't you?'

Without denying that either, he sat down on the edge of the bed and slowly filled his pipe.

'How did you find out?' he went on. 'Did you see him do it?'

He pointed to the window.

'No. I was telling you the truth. I always tell the truth. I can't lie, not because I can't abide lying, but because I blush when I do.'

'Did you really close the shutters?'

'I always do. The thing is, I sometimes used to find Victor in parts of the house where he shouldn't have been. He had a knack of moving around in complete silence, as if the air didn't even stir. It made me jump a few times, suddenly finding him next to me.'

Of course, he moved like a poacher! The same thing had suddenly occurred to Maigret when he was looking from the safe to the door and back again, but too late . . .

The secretary pointed out a bell in the corner of her bedroom.

'You see that. It was put in so Monsieur Fumal could call me at any time. Sometimes that was in the evening, sometimes pretty late at that. I had to get dressed and go over to see him because he'd have some urgent piece of work to give me, especially after business dinners. That was when I'd sometimes come upon Victor on the stairs.'

'Would he give you any explanation for being there?'

'No. He'd just give me a look.'

'What sort of look?'

'You know . . .'

It was true, Maigret probably did know, but he wanted to hear it from her all the same.

'There was a tacit complicity between everyone in the house. None of us liked our boss. We each had secrets, to a greater or lesser degree.'

'You have one to do with Félix.'

Confirming how easily she blushed, she went red up to her ears.

'What are you talking about?'

'The evening Fumal made you strip . . .'

She walked to the window and shut it.

'Have you talked to Félix about it?'

'No.'

'Are you going to?'

'What for? I'm just wondering why you put up with it.'

'Because I want us to get married.'

'And go and live in Giens!'

'What's the harm in that?'

What did she care about or want more: marrying Félix or being the landlady of an inn in the Loire?

'How were you getting the money?'

Émile Lentin was taking it out of petty cash. She must have had a ruse of her own.

'I can tell you, because there's nothing illegal about it.'

'Go ahead.'

'The director of Northern Butchers was interested in certain figures I had access to, because he could make a big profit on the side with them. It would take a long time to explain exactly how. As soon as I had the figures, I'd telegraph them to him, and every month he'd pay me quite a sizeable sum.'

'What about the other managers?'

'I'm sure everyone was stealing, but they didn't need any help from me.'

So, Fumal, the most mistrustful of men, the most ruthless of businessmen, was surrounded exclusively by people cheating him in one way or another. He spied on them, spent his life watching them, threatening them, making them feel the weight of his authority.

And yet a man stayed several nights a week in his own house without him knowing, came and went as he pleased, ate at his expense and didn't think twice about tiptoeing past the bedroom where he was asleep and taking money from petty cash.

His secretary was hand in glove with one of his managers.

And Monsieur Joseph must have made a bundle too, mustn't he? Not that they'd necessarily ever know; there was every chance that even the experts of the finance department wouldn't find anything.

To guarantee the services of a bodyguard, a loyal guard dog, he had saved a local poacher from prison. No doubt he called him up to his office too, of an evening, to give him confidential little assignments.

And yet of them all it was Victor who hated him the most. With a peasant's hatred, patient, tenacious, the same hatred that the poacher had nursed for years for the game-keeper whom he had ended up killing when the right moment came along.

Victor had waited for the right moment with Fumal too. Not just an opportunity to kill him, because he had any number of those every day. Or to kill him without being caught, but an opportunity to do so and set himself up for life into the bargain.

Wasn't it partly the sight of the empty safe, the missing fifteen million that had suddenly put Maigret on the right track?

He would analyse it all later. The elements were still all jumbled up in his mind.

The Luger played its part too.

'Was Victor in the war?'

'At an ammunition depot, near Moulins.'

'Where was he during the occupation?'

'In his village.'

The village had been occupied by the Germans. That was the sort of thing Victor would do too, get hold of one of their weapons during their retreat. Maybe he'd even hidden a stash in the woods.

'Why did you warn him?' Maigret asked reproachfully.

'Warn him about what?'

She blushed again, then caught herself doing so, which disarmed her.

'I talked to him when I went downstairs. He was standing at the bottom, looking worried.'

'Why?'

'I don't know. Maybe because the safe was being opened. Or because he heard you, or one of your men, say something that made him think you were on his trail.'

'What did you say to him exactly?'

'I said: You'd better make yourself scarce.'

'Why?'

'Because he did everyone a favour by killing Fumal.'

She seemed to be defying him to contradict her.

'Besides, I sensed you'd discover the truth. Afterwards it might be too late.'

'Admit that you were starting to feel nervous.'

'You suspected Félix and me. Well, Félix had a Luger too. He was part of the occupying forces in Germany. When he showed me the gun, which he'd kept as a souvenir, I said he had to get rid of it.'

'How long ago was that?'

'A year.'

'Why?'

'Because he's jealous. He has violent rages, and I was afraid he'd shoot me in one of them.'

She said this without blushing; in other words, she was telling the truth.

Every police station in Paris had been alerted. Squad cars would be criss-crossing the neighbourhood, passers-by would be being scrutinized on the pavements, bar and restaurant owners would be seeing officers lean in to have a quiet word in their ear.

'Can Victor drive?'

'I don't think so.'

The roads were being watched nonetheless. In a radius stretching far from Paris gendarmes would be setting up checkpoints and inspecting the occupants of every car.

Maigret felt useless. He had done everything in his power. It wasn't up to him now. To tell the truth, it was going to be more a matter of luck than police expertise now.

They were looking for one man out of millions, and he was determined not to be caught.

Maigret had botched it. He had figured it out too late. As he was heading to the door, Louise Bourges asked him:

'Do we have to stay here?'

'Until you're told otherwise. There'll be formalities to observe, maybe you'll need to answer some questions.'

In the courtyard Félix watched him suspiciously, then immediately went upstairs to find the young woman. Was he going to make a jealous scene because she had been ensconced in her room with Maigret?

Maigret left the building and made for the nearest bistro, the first one on Boulevard des Batignolles, where he had already taken refuge once.

The owner, who had a good memory, asked:

'Glass of beer?'

He shook his head. He didn't feel like beer today. The bar smelled of *marc de Bourgogne* and, despite the time, he ordered:

'A *marc*.'

He asked for a second and later, his mind elsewhere, a third.

It was strange that this drama had started at Saint-Fiacre, a tiny little village in the Allier, where he and Ferdinand Fumal had been born.

Maigret had been born in the chateau, or more precisely in one of its cottages, where his father was the estate manager.

Fumal was born in a butcher's shop, and his mother didn't wear underwear so as not to keep men waiting.

Victor was born in a hut in the woods, and his father ate crows and vermin.

Was that why Maigret felt he understood them?

Did he really want the manhunt to succeed and the former poacher to be sent to the gallows?

His thoughts were hazy. They were more like a series of images that filed through his mind as he stared at the cloudy mirror behind the bar's bottle-lined shelves.

Fumal had behaved aggressively towards Maigret because when they had been at school together, Maigret was the son of the estate manager, an educated man who represented the count in his dealings with the peasants.

Victor must have considered anyone who didn't roam the woods like him, anyone who lived in a proper house and wasn't in open conflict with the gendarmes and gamekeepers, an enemy.

Fumal had made the mistake of bringing him to Paris and shutting him away in that big stone box on Boulevard de Courcelles.

Hadn't Victor felt a prisoner there? Living alone in his

lodge like an animal in its burrow, hadn't he dreamed of the morning dew and game caught in traps?

He didn't have a rifle here, like in the woods, but he had brought his Luger with him, which he must have some-times stroked nostalgically.

'Same again, landlord.'

But he immediately shook his head.

'No!'

He didn't feel like drinking any more. No need. He had to finish the job he'd started, even if his heart wasn't in it, go back to his office at Quai des Orfèvres and oversee the search.

Quite apart from the fact that there was still an English-woman to be found!

9. The Search for the Missing Persons

The newspaper headline that best summed up the situation ran:

Double failure for the Police Judiciaire

The implication being:

Double failure for Maigret

A tourist had left a hotel in Saint-Lazare for no apparent reason, gone into a bar, come out of it, walked straight past a policeman, and then vanished into thin air.

A distinctive-looking man, who had not only murdered the king of the meat trade but also a gamekeeper, had walked out of a townhouse on Boulevard de Courcelles in broad daylight, at eleven in the morning, while the police and an examining magistrate were inspecting the premises. He may have been armed; he was definitely carrying fifteen million francs.

He had no known friends in Paris, no relatives, male or female.

And yet, just like Mrs Britt, he had disappeared in the city without leaving a trace.

Over the subsequent weeks, hundreds, if not thousands,

of policemen and gendarmes all over the country spent an incalculable number of hours searching for both these people.

In time, public feeling died down, but the men responsible for the nation's safety kept a pair of names and descriptions among all the other persons of interest in their notebooks.

For two years, nothing more was heard of the woman or the man.

Mrs Britt, the landlady from Kilburn Lane, was the first to be found, in perfect health, married and running a boarding house in a mining town in Australia.

Neither the French nor the British police could claim credit for finding her. By pure chance, that honour fell to someone who had been part of the same herd of tourists on the trip to Paris and then happened to take a trip to the Antipodes.

Mrs Britt didn't see fit to explain herself. No one could force her to either. She hadn't committed any crime or misdemeanour. All the obvious questions – how and where had she finally met the man of her life? Why had she left the hotel, then France, without a word to anyone? – all that was her business, and when journalists came to question her, she promptly showed them the door.

Things played out differently with Victor, and he also disappeared for longer. His name was a permanent fixture in policemen's and gendarmes' notebooks for five years.

One morning in November, however, as a crowd streamed off a mixed passenger and cargo ship from Panama, the Cherbourg harbour police noticed someone travelling third class who seemed unwell and had a crudely forged passport.

'Will you come this way?' one of the inspectors asked politely after a wink at his colleague.

'Why?'

'Just a formality.'

The man left the queue of passengers, went into an office and was shown to a chair.

'Name?'

'It's there in front of you. Henri Sauer.'

'Were you born in Strasbourg?'

'It says so in my passport.'

'Where did you go to school?'

'Well . . . in Strasbourg . . .'

'At Quai Saint-Nicolas school?'

The inspector reeled off a string of names of streets, squares, hotels, restaurants.

'It's so long ago . . .' sighed the man, his face bathed in sweat.

He must have caught a fever in the tropics, because his body suddenly started trembling convulsively.

'What's your name?'

'I've told you.'

'Your real name . . .'

Despite being so sickly, the man didn't give in, simply repeating the same story over and over.

'I know where you bought this passport in Panama. The trouble is, you see, you got ripped off. You obviously didn't go to school for long. As forgeries go, this couldn't be worse, and you're at least the tenth person to be caught.'

The policeman fetched other similar passports from a filing cabinet.

'Look. Your dealer in Panama is called Schwarz and he's an ex-convict. He really was born in Strasbourg . . . Not saying anything? Up to you! Give me your thumb . . .'

The policeman calmly took the suspect's fingerprints.

'What are you going to do with them?'

'Send them to Paris, where they'll know straight away who you are.'

'And in the meantime?'

'We'll keep you here, of course.'

The man looked at the glazed door, behind which some other policemen were chatting.

'In that case . . .' he sighed, defeated.

'Name?'

'Victor Ricou.'

Even after five years, that was enough to ring a bell. The inspector stood up, headed over to the filing cabinets again and eventually dug out a file.

'The Victor from Boulevard de Courcelles?'

Ten minutes later Maigret, who had just got to the office and was going through his post, was informed by telephone.

The following day, in the same office, Maigret found himself studying a wreck of a man, a broken creature who seemed to have given up all thought of defending himself.

'How did you get out of Paris?'

'I didn't. I stayed here for three months.'

'Where?'

'In a little hotel on Place d'Italie.'

Fascinated, Maigret asked how, with just a few minutes' head start, Victor had made it out of the neighbourhood when the police had been alerted immediately.

'I grabbed a delivery tricycle that was parked by the road, then no one paid any attention to me.'

After three months, he had made his way to Le Havre and secretly boarded a ship bound for Panama with the help of one of the crew.

'At first he told me it would cost me 500,000 francs. When we were on board, he demanded another 500,000. Then, before disembarking . . .'

'How much did he take in total?'

'Two million. Out there . . .'

Victor had planned to live in the countryside, but there wasn't any real countryside. It was virgin forest almost the moment you left the city. Disorientated, he had hung around seedy bars, got robbed again. His fifteen million hadn't lasted more than two years, and he had had to start working.

'I couldn't stand it any more. I had to come back . . .'

The newspapers, which had made such a fuss about him at the time, devoted three lines to his arrest, because everyone had forgotten about the Fumal case.

Victor didn't even have to go to court. As the preliminaries dragged on because the witnesses couldn't be found, he had time to die in the prison hospital at Fresnes, where Maigret was the only person to visit him, two or three times.